THE SECRET OF THE OLD CLOCHE

Agatha Christine Mystery Stories

Also by Leslie Stahlhut

The Borderlands of the Heart and Other Stories

THE SECRET OF THE OLD CLOCHE

Agatha Christine Mystery Stories

by

Leslie Stahlhut

COYOTE ARTS

Albuquerque, New Mexico

Cover design by Felicia Cedillos.
Interior design by Jordan Jones.

ISBN   978-1-58775-036-6 (paper)
         978-1-58775-037-3 (e-book)
Library of Congress Control Number: 2022949634

Coyote Arts LLC
PO Box 6690
Albuquerque, New Mexico 87197-6690 USA
coyote-arts.com

for

Betsy Louise Noble

1955–2013

who always let my third-grade self
sneak off with her copies of Nancy Drew

Contents

CHAPTER ONE

The Lost Relation

AGATHA BURST INTO the corporate headquarters of Agatha Christie World Tours waving the afternoon edition of *The Acorn Register.* "The Baileys don't even have the decency to wait for Amelia Dettmer to be buried before they try to shut down her animal rescue!"

"Amelia Dettmer died?" Lydia Bigelow, Agatha's mother, peered over the top of her glasses.

"The funeral is at two o'clock." Agatha plopped the newspaper on the dining table that served as her mother's desk.

Lydia looked over the top of her glasses again. "Oh my," she said, then moved the newspaper aside.

For as long as Agatha could remember her mother was either sitting at this table planning tours based on the life and work of her favorite author, Agatha Christie, or she was gone on one of the junkets she had organized.

Agatha turned to look out the window of the front room where there was a large oak. As a child she had spent hours gazing out this window imagining her future—one filled with travel and intrigue—not unlike the life she lived up until a few weeks ago.

But it took just one disastrous dinner to simultaneously end her career at The Agency and her cover job as a sales rep for Global Yarns.

Agatha picked up the newspaper and reread the article looking for a new clue. Her brow furrowed.

"Don't do that," Lydia said sharply.

"Don't do what? Read the paper?"

"Don't get smart with me, young lady. You can read the paper, but don't do that with your forehead. You'll get wrinkles," Lydia said.

"I'm not a 'young lady,' mother. I'm a middle-aged woman who needs a job while I get my new career off the ground." Tucked away in Agatha's suitcase was an invitation to design a crochet hat for Aneta Genova's new collection. It was the opportunity of a lifetime.

"Well you're not going to find it wrinkling your forehead."

Agatha flipped to the classified section to see if anyone still advertised jobs in the newspaper. There was a small notice for a "confidential job" opening. Someone who didn't want to be named was looking for an investigator. Maybe she could persuade whoever it was that a downsized yarn rep would be perfect for the position.

Lydia looked at her daughter. She knew she shouldn't say anything, but she was never good at stopping herself even when she knew better. "Have you thought of dying your hair one of those Easter egg colors like the young people do? It would cover the gray."

Agatha let out a long sigh, glared, and got back to the topic that preoccupied her. "It says here that a 'peculiar' term in Amelia Dettmer's will could end up shutting down Q-G-A-R-S-T!"

"It's pronounced "Q-Garst," Lydia corrected.

QGARST, short for "Quercus Grove Animal Rescue Society and Thrift," was Amelia Dettmer's life's work.

The "animal rescue society" referred to Amelia Dettmer's homestead where rescued animals were housed while they awaited placement in forever homes. The "thrift" referred to a converted Army Navy surplus store that was the fundraising arm of the non-profit animal rescue and was known for its unique and hard-to-find vintage items. But according to the article in *The Acorn*, thrift store sales weren't QGARST's main source of revenue.

Amelia Dettmer was.

"It will be a shame if a living relation to Amelia Dettmer can't be found. QGARST won't get the funds it needs to continue operations."

"That *would* be a shame," Lydia said.

Agatha couldn't tell if her mother was being sarcastic or had stopped listening and thought she should fill the pause with a well-intentioned, but meaningless, acknowledgement.

"If you were looking for a relation to Amelia Dettmer, where would you look?"

"Woodlawn Cemetery," Lydia chortled.

"Living relations, mother!"

Lydia looked over the top of her glasses as if she were looking into the past. "Do you remember Amelia's birthday celebrations?" she asked.

"Do I ever! I think Mr. Bailey ran for mayor just to try to shut them down! You know, there's never been a time in the history of Quercus Grove anyone by the name of Bailey was interested in anything that didn't make them money or advance their social standing."

"The Baileys aren't very well liked," Lydia said dryly.

"They aren't very likable. Mr. Bailey only ever uses his law degree to intimidate and harass, Mrs. Bailey is a social climber of the first order, and whoever said 'There's no such thing as a stupid question,' never had to sit next to their daughter Lynette. If a living relation to Amelia isn't found, the Baileys will get all of the buildings on Amelia's property condemned and razed before the flowers on her grave wilt."

Although Lydia found Agatha's speech tiresome, her sentiments about the Baileys were widely shared throughout Quercus Grove. The decades-long war they waged against Amelia had been the topic of many hushed conversations.

Born on May 7, Amelia's entry into the world was forever tied to the sinking of the *Lusitania.* Her immediate family had died when she was a child, and the animals she rescued were the only family she had or cared to have. A self-described "disaster baby," she celebrated her birthday by hosting a party to which every animal in Madison county was welcome.

Sitting just outside the city limits of Quercus Grove and the grasp of city inspectors and zoning laws, Amelia's property line abutted the Baileys'. Her annual birthday festivities—coupled with her year-round rescue mission—caused her yard- and house-proud neighbors immense distress.

This pleased Amelia enormously.

The Baileys did everything they could to disrupt the celebrations, but try as they might, the law did not reach beyond their fence.

Then, several years before Amelia's death, the Baileys abruptly stopped their harassment of the elderly woman and put their energies elsewhere. Mr. Bailey focused on his law practice, Mrs. Bailey tended her roses, and Lynette became a docent at QGHM&S—the Quercus Grove Historical Museum & Society.

Agatha's own memories of Amelia were fleeting. Encountering her in the store was like finding Mary Poppins in the pet food aisle stocking up on cat chow, dog chow, flea powder, and small treats for her family of rescues.

Amelia—like the weeds Mrs. Bailey worked so hard to eradicate from her yard—maintained a firm grip on life, caring for the wayward and unadoptable pets of Madison County.

Then, a month before Agatha's unexpected return to Quercus Grove, Amelia took ill.

She stayed in her home as long as she could, but was eventually admitted to the hospital. One day, she asked the nurse for a pen and paper, and as Amelia wrote what would be her last worldly communication her heart gave out.

All agreed on the first 20 letters of her final missive:

To whom it may concern: QG.

But whether the twenty-first letter was an "A" or an "H" was vigorously debated in "Hot Takes," a special community engagement section on the op-ed page that the new editor, Roscoe Edwards had introduced.

The QGARST camp was certain the letter was an "A," and Amelia was attempting to communicate an instruction about the rescue. The QGHM&S camp was certain the letter was an "H," and Amelia was trying to point to a holding in the Historical Museum & Society that would reveal who the relation referenced in the will was.

"What do you think Amelia was trying to say in her last note? People seem to think it contains a hidden message," said Agatha.

"Possibly." Lydia was annoyed at being interrupted yet again.

"Maybe it was a secret about the Baileys!"

"I don't know what there could be that isn't already in the public record."

"You don't think they have any secrets?" Agatha's work for The Agency had taught her that everyone has secrets.

"I didn't say that, but *The Acorn* has reported on every birthday party and luncheon the Baileys have attended for the past 50 years," Lydia said, "As for Amelia, her family's roots in Quercus Grove and Madison County are broad and deep. Her mother and father were both certified Pioneers of Quercus Grove. I don't know what there is to know about Amelia that hasn't been published in the newspaper or documented in her Pioneers application."

"That doesn't mean there isn't someone who doesn't know they're a relation."

Your father was a Pioneer of Quercus Grove, and when I married him, the Historical Society roped me into becoming the chair of the Pioneers Committee. One of my duties was to review every application ever approved. When I read Amelia's there wasn't any sign of a relation who might still be living.

"So what about Lynette Bailey's application? Is there anything interesting there?"

Agatha's interruptions were wearing on Lydia. "The most interesting thing about Lynette's application is that one was never submitted."

"If a living relation to Amelia Dettmer isn't found, it will be a disaster for QGARST. That isn't right!"

"It might not be right but it was Amelia's wish that a living relation be located. Now, I really need to work."

Agatha mused on the case of Amelia Dettmer. She knew finding the motivation was key. Usually what propelled a person to act was a personal grievance. What could Amelia's be?

Lydia tried to concentrate on her tour, but her thoughts kept straying to her only child. Why had Agatha—who had traveled the world selling yarn for twenty-five years—given it up and returned home to become a crochet designer? If she were destined to live out what remained of her life in Quercus Grove, why hadn't she just gotten married when she finished college and given Lydia the grandchildren she deserved?

She looked across the dining table that served as her desk. It had been in her late husband Ralph's family for over a hundred years. It was at this table she and Agatha had addressed and stamped envelopes for Agatha Christie World Tours, the business Lydia started from scratch after her husband Ralph's ill-fated business trip.

Maybe it was the hours they spent working together that made Agatha a world traveler. More than once they met when they were abroad. There was a quick lunch in Istanbul when one of Agatha's suppliers canceled a meeting as Lydia was arriving for an Orient Express Junket, an amazing dinner in

Casablanca when Agatha was scouting Moroccan sources for a line of specialty yarns while Lydia did research for a tour based on *Destination Unknown*, an underappreciated novel from Agatha Christie's *œuvre*, and a quick cup of coffee at the train station in Barcelona.

Whatever it was, Agatha was past the age she could give Lydia grandchildren without stealing them from someone else. And in the moments Lydia was honest with herself, she was content with her life. Everything was comfortable. She liked being able to take off and travel at a moment's notice.

"Where do you think Amelia Dettmer's relations could be?" Agatha said, "and don't say the cemetery!"

"I don't know about any relations. All I do know is…." Lydia stopped.

"Go on," Agatha was curious to learn anything that might reveal a clue.

"One day I was at the courthouse as the result of that dreadful Officer Hughes citing me for failure to come to a complete stop. My attorney, Marcus Hill, and I were outside the courtroom where my case was about to be heard, and he was consulting with some high-flying criminal defense attorney. I think her name was Carrie, or maybe it was Karen. Anyway, she's very famous. Amelia Dettmer walked right up to her while we were in the middle of the conference and told that attorney she had a problem that couldn't wait."

"I wonder why Amelia would need a criminal defense attorney?" Agatha mused.

"As I said before you interrupted, Amelia stopped her right there in the hall. The blood was rushing through my head over the shame of my unjust ticket, so I couldn't hear most of the conversation, but I did hear the attorney agree to come out to Amelia's house later that day."

"It would seem Amelia Dettmer had something quite pressing to attend to if she took the time to track down this lawyer at the courthouse," Agatha said.

"If I had been able to think, that would have been my thought exactly."

"So you got your ticket nearly a year ago, and that was about four years after the Baileys stopped harassing Amelia about her birthday celebrations."

Lydia peered over her glasses at her computer screen. "Look at the time!" she said, "I need to go."

"Go where?"

"Istanbul. A lovely woman I met at traffic school — Sophia Frickenstein — is coming on the junket with me."

"What junket?"

"The Orient Express!" Lydia said thoroughly aggravated with her daughter.

"When were you going to tell me about this?" Agatha asked.

"I was going to tell you when you walked in, but you wouldn't stop talking about Amelia Dettmer!"

"What do you know about this Frickenstein woman?"

"She's a Quercus Grove Pioneer on one side, Agatha. Just like you! Which reminds me…." Lydia reached in to her purse and handed Agatha a USB stick. "Here's all the information you'll need."

Agatha's eyes narrowed. "Information for what?"

"For the presentation I'm scheduled to give tomorrow, but can't because I'll be in Frankfurt." Her mother gathered up one last stack of papers.

"And where is this presentation taking place?" Agatha asked.

"At the Quercus Grove Hotel. It's the annual Quercus Grove Pioneers Application Form Workshop. It's the Historical Society's best attended luncheon."

"But I have a commission to design. And it has to be done in two weeks!"

"I'm only asking you to do two things. One is to deliver this presentation."

"What's the other?"

"The other what?"

"You said you were only asking me to do two things. One is the luncheon presentation. What's the other?"

Her mother gave her a look that was both piercing and faraway, "You need to watch M. Poirot while I'm gone."

Agatha was about to protest, but there was a knock at the door.

She opened it to find a tall, impeccably coiffed woman in a tweed suit clutching a coordinating purse.

"You're not Lydia!" the woman greeted her.

"No, I'm not. My mother will be right with you." Agatha replied.

"Oh, Lydia, I was so afraid I had gotten the wrong address when this stranger opened the door," the woman said.

"No need to worry, Sophia," Agatha's mother assured her friend. "We're going to have a grand time!" Then Lydia turned to her daughter, "Don't forget the luncheon!"

CHAPTER TWO

A Chance Meeting

"**D**ON'T FORGET THE luncheon!" Lydia's voice rang in Agatha's ears.

Maybe it was just a bad dream.

Agatha rubbed the sleep from her eyes and looked at the stack of boxes that served as a nightstand. The USB stick her mother handed her as she left for the airport was right next to it.

It wasn't a bad dream.

It was her life.

*   *   *

Agatha had listened skeptically when her financial planner explained the advantages of moving back to Quercus Grove. "Think of the money you'll save on rent!"

She broached the subject with her mother.

"I don't know." Lydia said. "Things have changed."

Agatha soon learned one of the things that had changed was her old room.

The canopy bed she spent two summers babysitting to save for—gone. In its place, a platform bed with graphic pillows that read MY HAPPY PLACE, ME TIME, and ALL YOU NEED IS LOVE AND A DOG!

Also gone were the pink strawberry shortcake walls. Now the room was painted in the latest neutrals with small pops of color here and there—a red vase, a pink flamingo, and a bright green bowl filled with small bits of paper. Agatha grabbed one of the pieces of paper when her mother wasn't looking.

"It never pays to kick a skunk." Hard to argue with that, she thought.

When they reached the third floor, Agatha found the tiny room where she hid as a child was smaller than she remembered. Furnished with a futon and dozens of cardboard boxes piled on top of each other, there was barely space to turn around.

"Can't I stay in the guest room?" Agatha asked.

"Don't be silly!" her mother said, "You're not a guest. You're family! Besides, I couldn't ask a guest to climb two flights stairs and stay in a little tiny room with all of these boxes!"

*   *   *

Agatha's thoughts were interrupted by a knock at the door.

"Yoo hoo!" It was Mildred.

Mildred Green had joined the household shortly after Agatha's father, Ralph Bigelow, mysteriously disappeared while away on business. When he was reported missing, authorities made an exhaustive search of the area where he was last seen, but neither he nor his briefcase were ever found. Back in Quercus Grove, a memorial service was held and the circumstances surrounding his demise were never mentioned again.

Soon after that, Lydia started Agatha Christie World Tours to "put dinner on the table," as she liked to say. Meanwhile, in Quercus Grove, Mildred kept both the house and Agatha in order.

Agatha, looked around the room that stored the remnants of her mother's life. Just weeks earlier she had been living the dream, her job as a yarn sales rep providing the cover she needed for her work at The Agency. She had her own apartment, one that overlooked a magnificent pool and was an easy walk to the train station. Then, after one too many glasses of wine at an ill-fated dinner, her life's work unraveled.

Now she was relegated to a small room on the third floor of the house her great great-grandfather built, in a town that never felt like home.

"Agatha?" Mildred said, "M. Poirot needs a walk."

"Okay, Mildred," she replied.

Once she was dressed, Agatha followed her nose to the kitchen where she found fresh coffee, hot pancakes, and a cranky dog.

"Grrr," M. Poirot greeted Agatha when she entered the room. A small brown rescue of undetermined breed, with wiry hair that hinted at a terrier ancestor, he weighed twelve pounds and loathed Agatha with all of his heart.

"My favorite," Agatha said as she helped herself to a plate of pancakes and a fresh mug of coffee.

Mildred smiled. "I thought you'd need a good breakfast to get you through the luncheon today."

"There must be at least a dozen people dying to become certified Quercus Grove Pioneers," Agatha said cheekily.

"You'd be surprised," Mildred said. "It's the biggest luncheon they have all year. With the new tablescape competition and Amelia Dettmer passing, it will probably be the best attended luncheon ever."

The thought of people fighting to get into the Historical Museum & Society luncheon amused Agatha. When she finished her breakfast, she and M. Poirot set out on his much awaited walk.

As they made their way around the block, the little dog sniffed each rock and plant in his path. He lingered at the yards of those dogs he counted among his friends while breezing past others that held no interest for him. Twice he lunged after a cat with whom he seemed to have an ongoing dispute.

"You're back early," Mildred said when they returned.

"Early? It took us half-an-hour to walk around the block!"

"You're a magician. It usually takes an hour. Oh," the older woman reached into the pocket of her apron, "this came for you in the mail yesterday."

Agatha eagerly opened the envelope. "The accessory design book I requested on interlibrary loan is in!" she said. "I'm going to go get it right now."

"While you're at it, can you return these?" Mildred said, handing her a stack of a half dozen books.

"Sure." Agatha packed up the returns, put on her bicycle helmet, and hopped on the orange five-speed beach cruiser she had picked up for a budget conscious $45 — it even had a basket! Then, as if she didn't have a care in the world, she set out for the library.

Agatha rode swiftly until she reached Main and Union. Then she got off her bike and briskly pushed it down the sidewalk all the way to the library, which—thanks to a bond initiative—was larger than she remembered.

A new wing had been added, and the clock tower and two water fountains had been restored.

Agatha loved libraries. She loved how cool they were in the summer, how warm they were in the winter, and how quiet they were no matter what the season. As a child, she especially loved having all of that information right at her finger tips, and it was under a table in the school library where she met her future best friend, Henryetta Richardson. Better known as "Hank," she had studied library science in college and was now the head librarian for Quercus Grove Public Library.

Agatha walked through the automatic glass doors and made a beeline for the library's public bulletin board—QGPL News Notes—and began reading.

There was a meeting of the genealogical society, a talk by the recently hired director of QGARST, and a meet-up of local knitters—crocheters, the posting said, were also welcome.

Agatha was midway through an announcement about a lecture Mrs. Bailey was giving on the preservation and care of heirloom roses when she felt the breeze of someone rushing past followed by the click of heels going up the marble stairs to the circulation desk. She looked to see who was responsible for the near miss only to find it was her old, alphabetical-order nemesis—Lynette Bailey.

Unless there was a nail salon squirreled away in the stacks, the fact Lynette was in the library at all was peculiar.

Agatha lingered at the bulletin board and read an announcement about the upcoming Chocolate & Coffee Festival. She arrived at the circulation desk just as there was a mid-morning rush with a line several people deep and only one library assistant to help.

Agatha didn't mind the wait, but Lynette did, and in her usual fashion, she tried to shout her way to the front.

"Excuse me," she said too loudly for a dog park, let alone a library. "I've been here almost five minutes. If I don't get the book I requested immediately, Officer Hughes will ticket my car!"

"I'm sorry ma'am," the assistant said, "but library policy is to serve people in the order they arrive."

"Don't you ma'am me, Miss whoever-you-are! I'll have you know...."

"Ms.," the assistant corrected her, "Ms. Taylor. Please use your indoor voice."

"Do you realize who my father is?" Lynette said. "He is the former mayor. He could have you fired."

"The rules of the library are the rules of the library," Ms. Taylor said coolly.

People in line murmured approvingly while Lynette crossed her arms and looked at the ceiling. She took a break from staring at the ceiling to survey the line behind her. She glared when she saw Agatha, then resumed her foot tapping and ceiling staring.

Just then, a second library assistant arrived. She called "next" and Lynette clicked to the counter. "If I get a ticket, it will be your fault," she greeted the clerk. Then Lynette explained how she had received a notice for a book she had requested on interlibrary loan, and it had arrived while she was out of town.

"Sorry," the assistant said after checking, "the book was sent back because you didn't pick it up."

"I was out of town," Lynette said, exasperated. "How could I pick it up when I wasn't here?"

"If I put in another request, it will be here Monday," the assistant offered.

"I can't wait that long." Lynette tried to peer around the assistant to get a look at the shelves.

"I better not have a ticket!" she finally said, making a quick turn that caused her to lose her balance. She recovered enough to stumble into Agatha.

"Watch where you're going," she snarled.

It's no wonder she is the center of so much talk, Agatha thought, but her thoughts were cut short when another patron nudged her shoulder.

"You're next."

Agatha set her mother's stack of books on the counter.

"Oooh, was this any good?" the assistant asked.

"Was what any good?" Agatha asked, curious.

"This book, *The Lawn Road Flats: Spies, Writers, and Artists.* It sounds interesting."

Agatha looked at the book the assistant held in her hands. It had a blue cover with a photo of a white apartment building.

"I don't know. My mother checked it out," she said. "Can I take a look at it?" The assistant handed the book back to Agatha who immediately opened it and read the flap.

After several paragraphs that explained nothing she got to this:

> A number of British artists, sculptors, and writers were drawn to the Flats, among them the sculptor and painter

Henry Moore; the novelist Nicholas Monsarrat; and the crime writer Agatha Christie who wrote her only spy novel *N or M?* in the Flats.

Whoever wrote the dust jacket copy did not know Agatha Christie's work or they would have known her spy novels numbered more than one and included *Murder in Mesopotamia, They Came to Baghdad,* and her mother's favorite, *Destination Unknown.*

Agatha imagined how her mother must have bristled when she read the blurb.

She handed the book back to the assistant along with the interlibrary loan notice she had received.

"*Accessory Design,*" the assistant said, "that sounds much more interesting than *A Centennial History of Quercus Grove in Madison County, 1805-1905,*" then she went to the interlibrary loan shelf.

Agatha wondered what gems the *Centennial History of Quercus Grove* might contain and scribbled the title on the back of an envelope. Soon the assistant returned from the hold shelf with Agatha's book.

"This was much easier than my last interlibrary loan request," the assistant said. "I dread seeing Miss Bailey when she comes in."

"She comes here often?" Agatha tried to hide her surprise.

"Yes," the assistant sighed. "She usually goes to the genealogy room. Before Miss Dettmer died, she was here once or twice a week, but since Miss Dettmer's death, Miss Bailey has been here almost every day. Except for whatever took her out of town and made her miss the interlibrary loan. Very strange…." the assistant's thoughts trailed off.

Agatha was surprised. Avoiding Lynette was one reason she spent so much time in the school library. She hoped the young woman would say more.

The assistant looked to either side, then lowered her voice, "The Baileys seem to be counting on getting Amelia Dettmer's property annexed to the city. I heard Mrs. Bailey tell Lynette, 'We'll get that eyesore razed as soon as the will is executed—and it's your job to see to it a living relation isn't found!'"

Agatha said nothing. Working for The Agency taught her that people who spoke freely to her, spoke freely to everyone. She knew anything she said might find its way back to the Baileys who, it seemed, thought Amelia Dettmer had a living relation. It also seemed they were doing what they could to make sure that any living relation didn't surface before the estate was settled.

* * *

With her mother's books returned, her own interlibrary loan completed, and a new clue to follow, Agatha glanced at the clock on the wall. It was quarter after eleven. The luncheon would be starting in less than an hour, and she hadn't even gone through the presentation or figured out what to wear.

I'd better hurry, she thought, or I'll be late.

"Thanks for your help," Agatha said, waving goodbye.

Once outside, Agatha sped off on her bike. By the time she got home she had thirty minutes to get ready.

She looked over the pioneer certificate application that was in the pile of papers her mother had left for her. The straight-line lineage chart was similar to notes she kept when she worked in the field. She didn't know why she never thought to disguise them as a family history.

As her computer scanned the thumb drive, Agatha scanned the open suitcase that served as her closet and pulled out a navy pant suit with ecru piping that always made her look vaguely professional.

She finished reviewing the slides, grabbed her bike helmet, and headed out the door.

"Have a good time," Mildred said.

It was a short ride to the Quercus Grove Hotel. When Agatha entered the lobby, she surveyed herself in a large mirror. She ran a comb through her hair, pulled out a vintage tube of bright red lipstick, and put some on. Then she made her way to the room where the luncheon was schedule to be held.

Mildred was right. The turnout was huge. There were at least fifty people waiting to get into the ballroom of the Quercus Grove Hotel.

Since she was a presenter, Agatha was able to breeze past the long line of people waiting to be seated and go to the front of the room where the table for the Quercus Grove Pioneers Committee had been set up. She was greeted by several people she hadn't seen since high school. There was her eleventh grade English teacher, a friend from third grade, and Marcus Hill. Maybe she'd be able to talk to him after the presentation and find out if he had any work she could do.

In addition to the Quercus Grove Pioneers Committee table where Agatha was seated, there were twelve ornately decorated tables, each designed to seat ten. Not only was every seat at every table filled, but dozens of people stood against the walls.

Agatha wondered what the fire chief would do if she caught wind of the size of the luncheon crowd. She didn't need to wonder long. Looking out onto the sea of faces she would be addressing, she saw the fire chief seated at the table with the Quercus Grove Fire Department's entry in the tablescape competition complete with fire trucks and roads.

Other departments of the city and county government were represented along with The Law Office of Marcus Hill and the Madison County Heirloom Rose Club.

The much disdained and despised Officer Steven Hughes headed the Quercus Grove Police Department's entry in the contest. After the fire chief made a determination that the standing guests could stay for the presentation, lunch was served. The QGHM&S president called the meeting to order, and a few items of society business were voted on among the members present. Then it was time for Agatha's presentation.

"Excuse me." It was an intern from the Historical Society. "I need to make an announcement."

He deftly moved to one side of Agatha as he grabbed the gavel next to the podium and banged it on the sound block. "Attention!" the intern said. "Attention." Once the room quieted down, he continued. "We have no more application forms. If you need additional applications, go to the Quercus Grove Pioneer FAQ at the QGHM&S website. Turn in your completed applications and supporting documents at the QGHM&S office. You can do that either in person or by mail. Are there any questions?"

He banged the gavel before anyone could raise a hand and passed it to Agatha.

She set it aside and dove into the welcoming speech.

"Good afternoon, fellow Quercus Grovians!" Was that even a word? she wondered belatedly. No one said anything, so she continued.

"Let's take Ferdinand Tunnel's pioneer application, submitted in 1907, as an example." Agatha went over the submission line by line. The audience listened, rapt by the intricacies of the form and the application process. When she came to the last slide people stood and clapped.

It was the first standing ovation of her life.

Pleased with how well it went, Agatha handed the gavel back to the president and took her seat.

The president banged the gavel and immediately called the meeting back to order. Then she turned her attention to the final item on the luncheon agenda. "I want to thank you all for being here today," she said, "It's time to announce the winners of the Quercus Grove Historical Museum & Society Pioneers Application Luncheon Inaugural Tablescape Competition!"

The intern handed an envelope to the president who opened it carefully. After a brief pause, she read the card aloud. "Honorable Mention goes to the Quercus Grove Fire Department!" There was vigorous applause, loud cheers, and a few whistles. The fire chief beamed.

When the noise subsided, the president was ready with the second envelope, "third place goes to the Oak Prairie Women's Club." More applause. The intern handed yet another envelope to the president, and the audience quieted down, "Second Place goes to the Madison County Heirloom Rose Club." This announcement was followed by a polite but much less robust response than the previous two.

Then the president opened the fourth and final envelope. "First place for the Quercus Grove Historical Museum & Society Pioneers Application Luncheon Inaugural Tablescape Competition goes to…" she adjusted her glasses, "the Quercus

Grove Police Department." Loud cheers erupted, but as the applause abated a lone voice of dissent arose.

"That's not fair!" It was Lynette Bailey. "You only gave the police department first prize because you don't want Steven Hughes to write you a ticket!"

The president banged the gavel. "Order," she said.

"Where are the judging sheets?" Lynette demanded.

"Order," the president repeated. The Historical Society intern having anticipated this moment was ready with a stack of papers which he handed to Lynette.

She grabbed the nearest chair and sat down to read them, her brow furrowed.

You'll get wrinkles, Agatha thought.

"The chair would entertain a motion to adjourn," the president said as she pounded the gavel.

"I move we adjourn," Agatha said.

"You don't have standing," Lynette interjected.

"We are adjourned!" the president said, banging the gavel a final time.

"That was quite a presentation you gave," a familiar voice broke through the noise of chairs being stacked and tables being bused.

It was Marcus Hill, her high school detention buddy.

"I've been trying to find someone with the skills needed to locate a living relation to Amelia Dettmer. I'm so desperate, I even placed a confidential ad in *The Acorn*," he admitted.

Agatha was about to explain that she hadn't prepared the presentation, but stopped herself. "How much does it pay?"

"Twelve hundred dollars," Marcus said. "I don't know if that's too much or not enough, but it's what I've got."

CHAPTER THREE

Racing the Storm

A FEW DAYS AFTER the luncheon, Agatha sat at the kitchen table with her laptop and a cup of coffee. When Marcus first offered her the job of finding a living relation to Amelia Dettmer, she thought it would be quick and easy. But now, a few days into her search, it wasn't turning out to be quick *or* easy. She poured herself another cup of coffee while M. Poirot ate his breakfast and occasionally snarled between bites.

"Agatha, do you have plans for today?" It was Mildred.

"Marcus Hill hired me to find Amelia Dettmer's living relation. I'm not having any luck finding clues on the Internet, so M. Poirot and I are going to ride out to St. James Cemetery to jump-start the investigation."

"Would you have time to stop by QGARST and drop this off?" Mildred pointed to a large paper grocery bag.

"Sure," Agatha said.

"So, you're working on the Dettmer case," Mildred paused. "Do you have any leads?"

Agatha's face clouded over. "I've eliminated a dozen potential relations, but the case is tougher than I expected."

"Don't let it get you down," Mildred said. "I don't think the CIA could unearth Amelia's secrets."

"Maybe the CIA couldn't, but I don't think anyone on the planet is nosier than I am — at least that's what you used to say!"

Mildred laughed. "You were very nosy." Her demeanor suddenly became serious. "You should go soon. The oak tree is picking up wind, and that means a storm is moving in. This time of year the weather can change on a dime." She snapped her fingers for emphasis.

Mildred was right. The weather, your life, it could all change on a dime.

*   *   *

But Agatha had a job to do, and inspecting Amelia Dettmer's grave was a good place to start. She always learned more when she looked at something for herself. Just this morning she found a bowling ball bag in her mother's decluttering empire. It wasn't exactly a lead, but it had plenty of room, a sturdy zipper, and it fit her budget.

Agatha plopped M. Poirot in her bicycle basket, and they reached QGARST in record time. When she opened the door, a bell announced their arrival.

Agatha set the bag Mildred had given her onto the counter. "Hello," she said, hoping someone would reply.

"Hello." An attractive middle-aged woman with graying locs emerged from behind a rack of vintage dresses, her right hand outstretched in greeting, "I'm Andrea Walker."

"Agatha Bigelow," she said extending her hand.

M. Poirot looked up at the two of them shaking hands and barked, annoyed at being ignored.

"And who is this?"

"M. Poirot."

A flicker of recognition flashed across Andrea's face, "You must be Agatha Christine!" she said. "I understand from your mother you crochet."

"I do. In fact, I have a design assignment that has me tied up in knots."

"What kind of assignment?"

"A crochet cap," Agatha said. "I thought designing would be easy, but I've spent the last week looking for inspiration."

"What about this?" Andrea pulled a worn pink beribboned cloche from behind the counter.

"It's perfect!" Agatha said enthusiastically. "Where did you find it?"

"About six weeks ago a famous organizer came to town. Her mantra is something like 'sparks joy.' She gave a lecture that sparked a lot of joy here at QGARST. Our donations have gone through the roof!"

"How much for the hat?"

"It *is* a genuine horsehair cloche…." Andrea began.

"How much?" Agatha interrupted.

"One hundred and fifty dollars."

Agatha gulped. Her financial planner told her to be cautious, but the cloche was tempting, and she did have a job.

Sort of.

"Do you take checks?" Agatha asked.

"Yes," Andrea said.

Anxious to ride out to the cemetery to work on the Dettmer case, she quickly wrote a check.

Andrea examined the document and handed it back to Agatha. "This is from a new account and doesn't have a number printed on it. I can't accept it," she said, "QGARST policy. There is a self-appointed ombudsman who looks over all of my work to make sure I dot every 'i' and cross every 't.' If I miss the slightest thing Lynette Bailey brings it to my attention and the board's."

How like Lynette, Agatha thought. "Do you take debit cards?"

"Yes, but the system is down. I'm waiting for a technician to come fix it."

Agatha felt like she was running out of time and options. "Can you hold the hat while I go to the bank?"

"Sure," Andrea said.

Agatha and M. Poirot made a beeline for the door and nearly ran into Lynette Bailey on their way out.

"Hey, you almost knocked me over," Lynette yelled.

"Sorry," Agatha said.

Not sorry, she thought.

When she reached the bank, Agatha discovered she could complete transactions at the ATM from the comfort of her bicycle. M. Poirot watched intently as she entered her PIN, and barked when a notice flashed on the screen that she had reached her daily $100 limit.

Fifty dollars short of what she needed, Agatha pedaled to the drive-through window.

"I need to make a withdrawal," she said to the intercom.

"This is the car lane," a voice replied. "You'll need to come inside."

"But...." Agatha stopped herself. She didn't have time to argue. She pedaled to the front of the bank, parked her bike, and grabbed M. Poirot. They were about to enter the bank when she saw the sign:

No Pets
Allowed
In Bank!
Service
Animals
Only!

Agatha grabbed her wallet from the bag and stuffed M. Poirot into it. Once inside she threw caution to the wind and wrote a check for $125. She could buy the hat along with a few skeins of yarn, and she would still have $25 in her account.

Hopefully, success would arrive before the bills did.

The teller looked at the check. Her hair was dyed one of those Easter egg colors her mother liked so well. "Is Agatha Christine your real name?"

"Yes," Agatha said.

"There's a famous author named, Agatha Christie. Are you related?"

"No," Agatha said, "But my mom is a big fan of her work."

"My grandmother read her books to me when I was a kid. I loved them. What's your favorite?"

None of them, would have been Agatha's honest answer. "*Cat Among the Pigeons,*" she said.

"I love that book!" the teller gushed. "After my grandma read it to me, I wanted to go to that school—what was the name of it?" The teller thought for a moment. "Meadowbank!"

Nothing like a pair of almost unsolved murders to make a school more inviting, Agatha thought. She felt her bag squirm.

The teller's eyes almost fell to Agatha's rambunctious purse. "How do you want your money?"

"Four twenties, two tens, and five fives," Agatha said.

The teller counted out the bills then put them in an envelope. "Good-bye, Agatha Christine," she said waving as Agatha left.

By the time Agatha and M. Poirot were out the door, the breeze Mildred saw stirring the top of the oak was a steady and sustained gust. It was into that gust she pedaled back to QGARST.

*　　*　　*

"I need that hat back," Lynette said, her eyes on Andrea as she pointed to the cloche.

"It's sold."

"If it's sold, why is it here?"

Andrea knew this precise situation was addressed somewhere in the QGARST Procedures Manual, and Lynette knew exactly which numbered paragraphs addressed it. "The payment processing system is down. I can only accept cash and checks right now, and the customer went to get cash."

Lynette's eyes narrowed.

Andrea sorted through the donation bag Agatha had brought in while Lynette tapped her foot.

She wore the strappy pink patent leather Manolo Blahniks she picked up on her last trip to QGARST—the one when she had dropped off the hat that she now wanted back.

"If you won't give it back, then you need to sell it to me."

"The hat is sold!"

"It can't be! It's still here."

"It's sold," Andrea said. "Trust me."

"How much did it sell for?"

"One hundred and fifty dollars." Andrea hoped she would lose interest.

Lynette reached into her purse. "Here's $175," she said, putting it on the counter in front of Andrea. "Now you have to sell it to me because that's $25 more than you were asking."

Andrea was trying to come up with a counterargument, when Agatha and M. Poirot burst through the door.

"I've got the money!" Agatha said, waving $150.

"You're too late," Lynette said, "I've got $175, so it's mine!" She laid the bills on the counter.

"Not quite," Andrea said.

"You have to take my offer," Lynette insisted.

"Only if I don't offer more!" Agatha reached into the envelope she got from the bank. "I see your $175 and raise you five!" Agatha set $180 on the counter in a pile next to Lynette's.

Lynette scowled then looked in her wallet. "185, 186, 187, 188. I see your five and raise you eight," she said setting thirteen dollars on her stack.

Agatha reached into the bank envelope and pulled out a five and a ten. "I see your eight and raise you seven!"

Lynette reached into her bra and pulled out a ten-dollar bill. "I see your seven and raise you three!"

Agatha countered with her last ten, "I see your three and raise you seven" she said, placing it on her pile.

The total was now $205.

Lynette emptied her purse onto the counter. Out spilled a phone, a tube of lipstick, and a stash of change that weighed at least two pounds. They waited while Lynette stacked the coins into piles, "I see your seven dollars and raise you $12.53!" Lynette said.

Agatha laid three five dollar bills on the counter. "I see your $12.53 and raise you ... $2.47!"

Andrea looked to Lynette to see if the bidding would continue. She was about to say "sold," when Lynette found a five dollar bill in her cellphone case.

"I see your $2.47 and raise you $2.53," she said coolly.

With the total at $222.53 Andrea looked back and forth between Agatha and Lynette. No one spoke, then Agatha pulled out her last five dollars. "I see your $2.53 and raise you $2.47."

For one very long moment, Andrea, Agatha, and Lynette stared at the two piles of money on the counter next to the well-worn hat.

Finally Andrea broke the silence. "Sold!"

Agatha's financial planner was going to kill her.

"That's not fair," Lynette said. "Wait until my father hears about this!" She grabbed her money, threw all of her things into her purse, and then slammed the door on her way out.

"That was interesting," Andrea said.

"Yes, it was."

Agatha looked at the time. The fifteen minutes she allotted had turned into an hour-and-a-half. In solving the problem of what to do for her design commission she had spent her way into another.

With just twenty-five dollars to her name, she now needed to find a living relation to Amelia Dettmer more than ever.

* * *

Agatha huffed and puffed into the increasingly stronger wind while M. Poirot sat in the basket, his nose tilted up into the stiff breeze. They rode past the butcher shop, the Historical Society Museum, and finally the Dairy Maid—a popular hamburger stand on the edge of town.

When they reached the entrance to St. James Cemetery, she surveyed the landscape. There was farmland to the north and west. Immediately south was a grove of oaks. That stand and others gave Quercus Grove its name. To the east was a farm, with a wide driveway, a barn, and a house made of bricks.

Agatha pulled her bike onto the platform of a gazebo in the center of the cemetery, secured M. Poirot's leash to the collar, and they began their tour.

They started at Amelia's grave. Most of the flower arrangements were wilted, but one stood out from the others. It was a large wreath of roses with a ribbon that read, "To Our Dearest Neighbor—from the Baileys."

"They left out 'whose property we want to annex so the buildings can be razed, leaving the rescue animals of Madison County homeless,'" Agatha said to M. Poirot. While she didn't like his snarls and general bad attitude, he did listen to her "soapbox lectures," as her mother called them, without complaint.

They didn't find any Dettmers buried near Amelia, but most peculiar to Agatha was the fact that Amelia—a Pioneer of Quercus Grove on both sides of her family—not only didn't seem to have a living relation, she didn't seem to have any dead ones either.

The wind picked up and the fast moving clouds blotted out the sun. M. Poirot was having none of Agatha's malingering. With one firm tug of his leash, he was off.

Agatha's entreaties for M. Poirot to come only made him run faster. Either that or her shouting made her run slower.

Agatha followed after the terrier to a forgotten corner of the cemetery where Agatha spied the name Dettmer on a marker nestled between Newmans and Hills.

Then, as she was about to reach him, a bolt of lightning struck nearby.

CHAPTER FOUR

An Interesting Story

M. POIROT RAN FASTER.

Rain fell in torrents, thunder shook the ground, and lightning filled the sky. Agatha's shoes were heavy with mud, her hair was plastered to her face, but the tricks she learned tailing foreign operatives helped her narrow the gap, and their journey ended when the terrier scampered into a barn.

Before Agatha could pick him up, M. Poirot began barking, as another door to the barn swung open.

An older woman stood in the doorway. She glanced at Agatha, then turned to M. Poirot.

"You look like a sweet doggy," she said to him.

M. Poirot shook as he wagged his tail.

"A very cold, very wet, very sweet doggy. Let me see if I can find something to warm you." The woman walked over to pile of blankets, selected one, and took M. Poirot from Agatha and wrapped him up. "What a wonderful dog you are," she said. M. Poirot shivered in agreement.

"Thank you for your help," Agatha said. "I'm Agatha Bigelow. We were out at the cemetery when...."

"Oh, Ralph's daughter," the women said. "Didn't you just move back to town?"

Agatha wondered if *The Acorn* had run a front page story about her return. She imagined the headline: AGENT LOSES TWO JOBS IN ONE DAY!!! WILL BE RETURNING TO QUERCUS GROVE TO LIVE THE REMAINDER OF HER LIFE IN IGNOMINY!!!

"I did." Agatha said. Although she shouldn't have been, she was always surprised at how quickly word traveled in a small town.

"I'm Eleanor Frickenstein," the woman said. "What a wonderful dog you are, M. Poirot," she cooed. Then she turned to Agatha, "So what brings you here?"

"The dog," Agatha pointed to M. Poirot who Eleanor had cradled in her arms. "We were at the cemetery and he decided it was time to leave." She shivered, "It sure has gotten cold."

"If the temperature keeps dropping," Eleanor said, "we'll probably get hail."

"I thought we had time to make it back to town, but here we are," Agatha said, grateful to be in the shelter and relative warmth of the barn instead of waiting out the storm huddled on the cemetery gazebo with a cold, wet, angry dog.

"What brought you out to the cemetery?"

Agatha didn't know how much she should say. While Amelia Dettmer's death and the peculiar term of her will were public knowledge, Agatha's involvement in finding a living relation was not. She decided to tell what she thought of as "truth scraps."

No out and out lies that would be hard to remember, but pieces of the truth that didn't reveal the whole story. "I used to ride my bike out here as a kid, and I thought it might be fun."

"Well, it's nice to have company," said Eleanor.

"M. Poirot doesn't usually take to strangers the way he's taken to you," Agatha said.

"Oh, we're not strangers," Eleanor said. "We're just friends who hadn't met!"

The trio stood in silence watching as the rain continued to come down in sheets.

Eleanor walked over to the still open barn door. "This storm looks like it's here to stay awhile."

Agatha and M. Poirot walked to the door where Eleanor stood and looked out. In the distance they could see a lonely oak in the middle of the field. It had been split by lightning.

"Maybe we should stand further back," Agatha suggested. "My teacher Mrs. Lee used to say 'When thunder roars, go indoors.'"

"What an excellent idea!" Eleanor said. "Why don't the two of you come in the house and sit out the storm with me? M. Poirot can have a bowl of chicken soup, and you and I can have a cup of tea."

M. Poirot's ears perked up and he wagged his tail at the word chicken.

Agatha wanted to decline the offer, but it didn't seem polite to make Eleanor wait in the barn with them while the storm raged. "I don't want to be any trouble."

Eleanor waved off the suggestion. "You're no trouble. My sweet little Annie—she was an adorable terrier mix—recently passed away. It will do me good to have a dog in the house again."

Then she stopped as if she just remembered something. "Isn't your mother the woman who arranges the Agatha Christie tours?"

"Yes, she is," Agatha said.

"That explains why a woman as young as you has such an old-fashioned name."

When Agatha turned fifty, she had stopped thinking of herself as young. There were moments when she felt youthful—but they were just moments. They didn't last long.

"Do you know my mother?" Agatha asked.

"Only by reputation," Eleanor said, "but my sister-in-law, Sophia, met her at traffic school. Before Sophia met your mother she talked of nothing but how awful 'that Officer Hughes,' was. After traffic school, she sang a completely different tune. She said that even though Officer Hughes was in the wrong, writing her that ticket was kismet. She went to the library and read every Agatha Christie book they have. She's been looking forward to going on one of those tours your mother puts together since the moment they met."

"They left on one the other day," Agatha said.

"Really?" the older woman said. "I would have thought she or my brother Edward would have mentioned it. Of course," Eleanor seemed as if she were about to say something then thought better of it, "I've been busy with the farm."

There was another loud clap of thunder that left M. Poirot trembling. "Let's go in the house," Eleanor said. Agatha and M. Poirot followed their hostess through the barn past some empty stalls to another door that let them out a few feet from the house. The three of them scrambled up a set of steps that led up to a covered porch.

"It sure is a lot cooler now than it was when M. Poirot and I set out on our adventure," Agatha said.

"I saw the wind stirring in the top of that line of trees this morning," Eleanor said, pointing to a windbreak, "and I knew that something was on the way. It's like that this time of year." M. Poirot shivered while Agatha removed her muddy shoes. Eleanor slipped into a pair of woolen clogs and ushered them into the kitchen, then disappeared down a long hall and returned with fresh towels. Agatha dried herself off while their efficient hostess took a towel to M. Poirot who was soaked to the skin after the trek from the barn to the house.

Eleanor's kitchen was an oasis of calm in the center of the storm raging outside. Suddenly, a shadow raced from the kitchen out another door. "Oscar," that's no way to behave," Eleanor admonished, "I've brought you guests." Eleanor turned to Agatha, "Oscar is my cat."

Eventually, curiosity got the better of Oscar, and he returned to the kitchen. While he and M. Poirot regarded each other with suspicion, Eleanor made a pot of tea and warmed a bowl of homemade chicken soup for M. Poirot. She was tall like her sister-in-law Sophia, but her face had a more serious expression, and her hair was more gray. It was clear by the way she carried herself that despite sharing a last name and living in the same county, her life and Sophia's were quite different.

Agatha appreciated Eleanor's cordial welcome which included a plateful of cookies along with a steaming mug of tea. "It's nice of you to invite us in the way you have."

"It's a pleasure for me, and even Oscar," Eleanor assured her. "We don't get a lot of company unless I hire work done.

I get into Quercus Grove most weeks, but it isn't often I get to share my home with visitors, Ms. Bigelow."

"Oh, please call me Agatha. Ms. Bigelow makes me feel like I'm at work."

Soon Eleanor and Agatha were talking as if they had known each other for years. Meanwhile, M. Poirot devoured the soup, and Eleanor insisted on fixing him a second serving. Agatha could not remember the last time she enjoyed meeting anyone so much. It was almost as if she were back with The Agency making a contact in a new yarn shop.

"Where did you get this?" Agatha asked, noticing a pot holder Eleanor had used to maneuver the bowl of soup she heated for M. Poirot.

"Oh, that," Eleanor said dismissively, "I made it."

"It's a very interesting piece. May I look at it more closely?"

"By all means," Eleanor encouraged her.

The potholder was a simple square made from wool and then felted. Because of how perfectly square it was, Agatha suspected it had been crocheted in the round.

"So this is felted, right?"

"Yes," Eleanor said, "I used an Australian Merino wool. I love the colors of the Peruvian wools, but it's hard to beat Merino wool for felting. The shorter cuticle length makes it felt so much more quickly." She stopped suddenly. "If I'm boring you, please don't be shy about asking me to stop."

"Oh, I'm not bored," Agatha said. "As you might have heard, I worked as a sales rep for a yarn company for a number of years." Agatha paused to see if Eleanor's expression would give anything away. It didn't. "The yarn company I worked for got bought out by another one so, I ended up retiring a few weeks ago. Now I'm home to try my hand at crochet design."

"Really? That sounds interesting. Would you like to see my crochet collection?"

"Certainly!" Agatha could not believe her good fortune. The worst of the storm had passed, but it was still raining, and Agatha and M. Poirot were going to need to stay put for at least another hour before they could think about heading back to town.

Eleanor's living room was even more inviting than the kitchen, and it housed an eclectic array of furniture and curios that looked like they could have been taken straight from the Quercus Grove Historical Museum.

There was so much to see, Agatha didn't know where to look first. Then her eyes landed on an upright piano with a crazy quilt piano scarf across the top of it. "This is beautiful!" Agatha gasped.

"Isn't it?" Eleanor smiled knowingly. "It was made by my Great Aunt Eleanor—I was named for her. In 1876, she and her brother Hilbert traveled to the Centennial Exhibition in Philadelphia. Like a lot of women of her time she was inspired by the English embroidery and Japanese art exhibits, and the result was this crazy quilt piano scarf."

Agatha surveyed the intricate piecing and the elaborate topstitching. There were rows of familiar feather and herringbone designs with flowers crafted from blanket stitches and French knots, but there were also unusual combinations Agatha had not seen before. "This is amazing work," she said.

"I'm glad to know there are young people who appreciate crafting. These days everyone thinks the answer to any problem is to make a machine to do it. When it comes to harvesting crops I'm one of them, but I do love handwork."

"May I take a photo?" Agatha asked.

"Certainly," Eleanor said.

Agatha was glad to find her cellphone in her back pocket. With the way her life had gone the past few weeks she wouldn't have been surprised if it had fallen into the muddy field as she ran after M. Poirot.

After taking pictures of the piano scarf, she finally saw what was on top of it. To her shock, she found herself looking at a sepia photograph of a young woman wearing what looked to be the exact hat she had bought at QGARST less than two hours earlier. The one tucked away in the bowling ball bag hanging off the handlebar of her bicycle which she had parked underneath the gazebo at St. James.

Hopefully no one was at the cemetery to steal the bag, her identity, and the hat that she had mortgaged her immediate future to buy.

"What a lovely photo," Agatha said, hoping the curiosity she felt had not crept into her voice. She learned long ago, the best way to feign indifference was to actually be indifferent, but at the moment all she could hear was the blood rushing through her head as she recognized that she was hot on the trail of a mystery. She turned to her hostess, "and what a lovely hat."

"It's very distinctive. The woman wearing the hat is, or I guess I should say *was*, Amelia Dettmer. The woman in the floral print standing next to her is Sevilla. She's the one who made that hat for Amelia on the occasion of her twenty-first birthday. My mother said there was quite a story to it.

What story? Agatha wondered. Maybe it would explain the Baileys' interest in getting the hat back. "You've piqued my curiosity," she said aloud.

"Oh, you're saying that to be polite."

"Not true!" Agatha insisted, "You can ask my mother when she gets back to town. I never say anything to be polite. She considers it a fault of mine," Agatha said with a smile.

Eleanor laughed and then her face grew quite serious. "The truth isn't always polite," she observed.

As if on cue, M. Poirot began to bark. "I wonder what's gotten into him," Agatha said. She looked out the window where he stood guard, but aside from the wind and the rain, there did not seem to be anything out of the ordinary.

"So what about, Sevilla?" Agatha said, trying to steer the conversation back to the picture, the hat, and the story. "She looks like she was an interesting woman."

"She was," Eleanor said. "In fact, she was one of four women in her class to graduate from Quercus Grove High School. At the time, it wasn't uncommon for a young woman's father to insist she stay at home to work on the farm once she finished the eighth grade. That," the woman continued, "was what happened to Amelia."

"But, I thought Amelia's father died when she was a child," Agatha said.

"He did." Eleanor paused as if she weren't sure she should say anything. "But there was a peculiar term in his will, and it stopped Amelia from going to high school."

"It seems 'peculiar' runs in the family."

"Indeed it does," Eleanor said. "Indeed it does."

CHAPTER FIVE

A Conference

"**A**RE YOU SURE you don't want a ride to the cemetery?" Eleanor asked.

"Thank you, but I need to walk off this mud," Agatha said looking at her shoes. "I also want to make certain M. Poirot is good and tired."

"If you're sure...." Eleanor said.

"I'm sure." With his leash firmly in her grip, Agatha and M. Poirot set out on the road that ran alongside the field they had run through earlier. When they reached the entrance to the cemetery, the mud on Agatha's shoes was gone and all that remained were impressive dirt stains. M. Poirot, still determined to get home, pulled at his leash dragging Agatha toward the gazebo and her bike.

He was ready to get into the basket and go.

Agatha was pleased to find that, even though rain had been blown onto the gazebo, everything in her bag was dry. She hoisted M. Poirot into the basket and they set out for home. As they prepared to make a left onto the road back to town, a burgundy sedan turned into the cemetery narrowly missing them. There was a couple in the car who appeared to be arguing, but the windows were up, and she was unable to hear what they were saying.

Agatha's suspicions were aroused. Other than adventure seekers who had read the rumors of the Ghost of St. James Cemetery, there weren't many out-of-towners who stopped by, and even fewer who did so after a thunderstorm. She watched as the car parked near Amelia Dettmer's grave, and the couple got out of the car. The woman teetered on a pair of heels that weren't suited for tromping in the newly muddied earth while the man walked with his hands in his pockets looking like he was afraid a ghost would ambush him as they made their way to the grave.

Tired of waiting, M. Poirot barked at her. He was ready to go.

Reluctantly, Agatha turned west and headed back to town. As she dodged puddles and downed tree branches she decided her first stop — muddy shoes, wet dog, and all — had to be Marcus Hill's office.

"Front Door Open," a woman's voice announced their arrival.

"What was that?" Agatha said, looking over her shoulder.

"That's our new alarm system," Marcus's paralegal said.

M. Poirot squirmed until Agatha put down and ran straight to Claudia. He made a graceful turn, then sat at her feet and barked.

"It's good to see you too," she said reaching into a drawer to get him a treat. He took it from her outstretched palm and headed to a corner where he could chew without being disturbed. "You look like you got caught in the rainstorm," she said smiling.

"We did, and now I need to see Marcus, ASAP. We came across a clue that might be important."

"Can it wait fifteen minutes? He's in a meeting with a client."

"Sure." Agatha hadn't come this far to turn back now. She had exhausted the few leads she'd had in the Amelia Dettmer case, so she was glad there was a new clue to follow.

Agatha watched the clock for what felt like hours as she looked over her newly acquired crochet "inspo." How had she left the house without a tape measure? Or yarn? Or a hook?

Agatha was engrossed in the new hat, when Marcus opened the door to his office, "Hi Agatha. I can see you now."

"I'm glad you could fit me into your schedule," Agatha teased. Busy with his treat, M. Poirot stayed in the corner, not even looking up as she was ushered into Marcus's office.

"I had an adventure," Agatha told Marcus once the office door was shut.

"I hope it relates to the Amelia Dettmer situation," Marcus said. "The fiends are starting to come out of the woodwork. The story of Amelia Dettmer's will was picked up by one of those tabloid television shows, and now everyone with even the most tangential connection to Quercus Grove is calling my office."

"Is that why you're so busy?" Agatha grabbed a handful of the foiled wrapped chocolate candies in a dish on the corner of his desk. "I missed lunch," she explained.

"As a matter of fact, it is. I can't be showing my hand to anyone at this point. With everyone in town for Chocolate &

Festival and the news of the Dettmer estate, the town is crawling with people looking to learn any detail they can use to lie their way into the will."

"I wonder why? They don't get the money, QGARST does."

"That's true, but animal rights activists are not a laid back group of people. They tend to be older, female, have pets they love, and are unwilling to take 'no' for an answer. Also, a number of them are near the end of their lives, they don't feel they have anything left to lose, and this is the hill they want to die on. In fact, that's what the last potential client said to me."

Agatha popped another piece of chocolate into her mouth. "Back to my adventure. I was thinking about what my mother said when I asked her where she would look for Amelia's relations. She said Woodlawn cemetery." Marcus unsuccessfully tried to suppress a laugh. "I did a little research," Agatha continued, "and she was onto something, but my investigation took me out to St. James — not Woodlawn."

Marcus raised his eyebrows. St. James Cemetery was a small plot of land east of town populated mostly by Pioneers of Quercus Grove, and even among the pioneers, it was a small subset. Not too many newcomers — anyone whose family arrived in Madison County after 1860 — were buried there.

"Besides Amelia, I was only able to find one other Dettmer in the whole place, but I didn't get to document it because it was pouring rain, and I was chasing after M. Poirot. Then he found a break in the fence and made a mad dash across a field. We just missed being hit by lightning and took refuge in a barn which is how we met Eleanor Frickenstein."

"How is Eleanor?" Marcus asked.

"You know her?"

"Our paths have crossed."

"Anything to do with traffic school?" she asked mischievously.

"Agatha, I can't discuss my clients with you unless it's related to investigative work for which I have specifically hired you."

"Right, boss," Agatha said winking at him. "She seemed preoccupied, but otherwise in good spirits. Her sister-in-law and my mother met at traffic school after each of them had been cited by Steven Hughes. I understand my mother got ticketed for not coming to a complete stop, which I have been told was a completely bogus charge. That is NOT coming from you!"

"Your mother was livid."

"Where was I?" Agatha paused to collect her thoughts.

"Oh, yes, in addition to running the family farm, Eleanor is also the keeper of the family heirlooms, and when I was there I noticed an exquisite crazy quilt piano scarf on an upright piano. The piano and the piano scarf have been in the family since the 1880s. The piano is just a piano, but the scarf is really beautiful. So beautiful I almost didn't notice the photograph right on top of it."

Agatha looked in her bag and pulled out the cloche with a flourish. "See this hat?" she put it on Marcus's desk.

"Yes," Marcus said cautiously.

"Have you ever seen it before?"

"No."

"Neither had I." Agatha popped another piece of chocolate in her mouth. "I bought it today for $225 which is another story altogether."

"I thought you were broke," Marcus said.

"I am. But I needed inspiration. The hat was in storage at the Baileys' house for years. Then the 'sparks joy' lady came to town, gave a lecture, and all of Quercus Grove decluttered their closets. Most of it ended up at QGARST."

"This is going to make sense soon, right?"

"Yes," Agatha assured him. "After I chased M. Poirot across the field, he ran into Eleanor's barn. She invited us to ride out the storm. Then she asked if I wanted to see her crochet collection. I said yes, and that's when I found a photo on the piano I mentioned earlier. It was of Amelia as a young woman and she was wearing this exact hat!" Agatha pointed to the cloche for emphasis. "Eleanor said a woman named Sevilla made this hat for Amelia's twenty-first birthday and that there's a story to it."

"Really?" Now Marcus was intrigued. "I don't know of any Sevillas in Quercus Grove. It's an unusual enough name, I would remember it if I had come across it."

"Exactly!" Agatha said, stuffing still more chocolate into her mouth. "I've been reading up on the Pioneers of Quercus Grove, and I haven't found her—yet—but maybe she and Amelia are related. Then she would *have* to be a pioneer on at least one side of her family, because Amelia was a pioneer on both sides!"

"I'm not sure how this is a breakthrough," Marcus said, not as impressed with either of Agatha's finds as she was. "If I understand correctly, the facts of the case are as follows: you paid way too much for a hat the Baileys donated to QGARST, and then after getting caught in a thunderstorm and chasing M. Poirot across a field, you ended up at Eleanor Frickenstein's house. There you saw a picture of a woman wearing a hat like this one," Marcus picked up the cloche, "and Eleanor told you the photo was of Amelia and a woman named Sevilla who might or might not have been related to Amelia Dettmer."

"You have all the facts right, but you're ignoring the story." Agatha retrieved the hat from Marcus's desk, "I know the answer is right here in Madison County, and I wouldn't be the least bit surprised if the Baileys know something they aren't telling."

"I doubt you'll be able to get them to tell you."

"What I need to do is look at the cemetery records down at the Quercus Grove Historical Museum & Society," Agatha said, her mind moving forward with her plans.

"Lynette and her mother volunteer there," Marcus said. "They've been very active with QGHM&S since Mr. Bailey stepped down as mayor. I guess not harassing Amelia freed up a lot of time."

"Or, maybe the two things are related." Just then, Agatha heard a familiar sniff at the door, followed by a bark.

"Sounds like M. Poirot is ready to go," Marcus offered, "and just in time. I have a 4:30 appointment."

"Kind of late in the day, isn't it?"

"It is," Marcus said, "but it's an old friend from law school, and he insisted the appointment couldn't wait."

Agatha grabbed the cloche, stuffed it in her bag, and opened the door. M. Poirot was at her feet and almost looked like he was glad to see her. The two of them said their good-byes to Claudia and were on their way. Right now she and M. Poirot both needed a good bath, and she had work to do.

CHAPTER SIX

An Unpleasant Encounter

T HE DAYS WERE going by at light speed and, despite her efforts, Agatha wasn't making any progress with the Dettmer case. It seemed every lead she followed took her to a new dead end.

Not only that, the crochet hat design deadline loomed on the horizon like a storm cloud waiting to rain on whatever parade dared cross its path. Agatha felt more stress in her retirement than she did when she worked two full-time jobs. Now both the Dettmer case and her crochet design project were at a standstill.

Meanwhile, with Lydia five thousand miles away somewhere in the Balkans, Mildred was making remarkable progress on the decluttering project. It seemed she was always in Agatha's room sorting through boxes, finding things Agatha hadn't known existed, and unearthing old favorites.

Just the day before Mildred had unpacked a shelf's worth of Nancy Drew books. As a result, Agatha was groggy-eyed from staying up past midnight reacquainting herself with Nancy's adventures. M. Poirot had snored through *The Secret of the Old Clock* and run in his dreams all the way through *Nancy's Mysterious Letter.* Finally, just before the town clock was about to strike two, Agatha fell asleep.

"You're worrying about the Dettmer case, aren't you?" Mildred said to Agatha one morning as M. Poirot picked over the remnants of his breakfast and Agatha nursed a third cup of coffee. "You shouldn't take it so much to heart," the older woman said topping off Agatha's nearly full cup. "If it were truly important, Amelia Dettmer would have named the relation in her will. I wouldn't be surprised if she just wanted to stir up trouble."

"I have been thinking about the Dettmer case," Agatha admitted. "It's hard not to when so much is on the line for the animals of Madison County. I was so sure I could figure it out."

"I think you need to take a break and then perhaps you'll have some inspiration. You should do something to take your mind off of it. Why," Mildred said slyly, "you could drop this off at QGARST!" She set a bag filled with tchotchkes and odd bits of memorabilia in front of Agatha. "Maybe then you'll be able to work on the hat you're supposed to be designing."

"You're right," Agatha said laughing.

*   *   *

When Agatha and M. Poirot got to QGARST, every space in the bike rack nearest the store was in use, so Agatha was forced to park near a new-to-her salon called the Cutting Edge. Just as she got her bike locked, a customer with hair dyed in graded shades of pink walked out. Maybe, Agatha thought, she *should* color her hair. M. Poirot, however, didn't have time for Agatha's reverie. He was impatient to get on with their errands, and he tugged at his leash until Agatha relented. They walked into QGARST just in time to hear a familiar voice.

"Listen, Angela, you need to give the hat back to me. My mother said she never meant to put it in the donation bag, and my father said…." Lynette was interrupted by the tinkling of the bell when the door opened. Lynette and Andrea both turned to look. "Oh, it's you!" Lynette said to Agatha, in an angrier voice than she had used when she was talking to the mysterious Angela. "I want my hat back!"

"Hello to you, too!" Agatha said.

"Did you hear me?" Lynette asked.

"Only the dead can't hear you," Agatha said.

"Well?" Lynette said.

"Well, what?"

"When are you going to give me back my hat?"

"Never. It's my hat now, and I have the receipt to prove it," Agatha said.

"My father said…."

"Wait," Agatha held up a hand, fished a notebook from her bag, and with a pen poised over a fresh page prepared to record any and all bits of wisdom Lynette was about to share.

"I'm not going to tell you! You're not even my father's client! If you want his advice, you can pay for it!" With that, she grabbed a bag with a purchase she had made and flounced out of the shop.

"Isn't that special?" Andrea said as Lynette made her exit.

"Whose Angela?" Agatha asked.

"I don't know who 'Angela' is, but it seems Lynette thinks that's my name."

*   *   *

With the errand done, Agatha and M. Poirot headed to the salon to retrieve her bike. She had read that walking outdoors improved creativity, and with both the Amelia Dettmer case and her crochet hat design at a standstill, something needed to change. So while she pushed her bike along the sidewalk, a securely leashed M. Poirot trotted next to her as they made their way to the park.

The long walk from QGARST to the park was made longer by the fact M. Poirot needed to sniff every corner and crevice. He didn't walk past a leaf, flower, or piece of garbage without inspecting it. There was nothing about which he was not curious, and he stopped frequently and cocked his head as if he were trying to eavesdrop on a conversation.

While M. Poirot was busy with his outward explorations, Agatha's mind wandered to the cloche she had purchased. She thought the decorative stitches worked on the surface were intriguing and wondered how difficult it would be to replicate the effect on the hat she was designing in her head. She was considering how to work double treble stitches in a spiral when her thoughts were interrupted.

M. Poirot growled softly and stood at attention, both ears pointing straight up. Agatha followed his gaze and saw Lynette with her mother's Great Dane, Peaches. They were already in the park, and It was clear, even from a distance, the dog was in charge.

Agatha put M. Poirot in the basket to avoid a confrontation with Mrs. Bailey's dog. She hoped the terrier would cooperate with her effort to make an escape, and although he did, Lynette did not.

"Peaches, no! Bad dog!"

How like Lynette, Agatha thought, to think you could get anyone's cooperation by yelling insults at them.

Then Lynette put her hand to her forehead to shade her face, "Agatha, is that you?" She didn't wait for an answer. "It is you!" Lynette pulled on Peaches' leash as she clicked her way over in what appeared to be her dog-walking heels.

The dog countered by standing her ground, which caught her substitute mistress off guard. After a series of awkward gyrations, Lynette was forced to let go of the leash to avoid falling on her face.

Surprised she had gotten away, Peaches made a lap around the park then ran toward the swings and slides where children were playing. Lynette trailed after the dog, limping along in her high-heeled sandals that did not seem up to the job of walking a Chihuahua, let alone a Great Dane.

Lynette's previously perfectly coiffed hair was beginning to come undone. The curls, having been lacquered in place to within an inch of their life, began to loosen while beads of sweat showed on her face.

"Peaches, come!" Lynette yelled. "Peaches, get back here… now!" The Great Dane ignored the threats and instead — to the delight of the children — galloped around the playground, inadvertently pushing one little boy on a swing even higher. He clapped his hands in appreciation.

"I need to talk to you," Lynette shouted as she neared Agatha and M. Poirot. "This is all your fault." She shook her finger as she puffed past them on the way to the playground. M. Poirot, who had been sitting in Agatha's arms, quietly growled.

When Lynette reached the swings, it turned out she had no plan to get Peaches to come back to her other than yelling "you stupid dog!" She gingerly stepped onto the rubber mats that had replaced all of the sand and teetered toward Peaches who was exhausted from her romp.

The large dog had paused to pant and visit with the children she had been entertaining, allowing Lynette to grab the trailing end of the leash.

"Bad dog, Peaches. Bad dog," Lynette said. Then pulling as hard as she could, she clicked her way back to Agatha and M. Poirot with Peaches in tow.

"What've you done with the hat?" Lynette asked, panting.

M. Poirot cautiously poked his head out from Agatha's bag to look at the Great Dane.

"I'm sorry, what did you say?" Agatha pretended she hadn't heard.

"I asked you what you did with the hat. I don't know why you want it so badly."

Anymore than I know why *you* want it so badly, Agatha thought.

Lynette held out a hand to admire her nails, then wrinkled her nose. "I think Diana missed a spot."

Agatha peered at Lynette's nails. "They look nice to me."

Lynette wrinkled her nose still more as she looked at Agatha's hands, "Not to be rude, but what would you know about manicures?"

"Woof," Peaches barked and raised her head as if to invite M. Poirot to play. M. Poirot continued to regard Peaches with equal parts suspicion, caution, and curiosity.

"What were we talking about?" Lynette asked. "Oh, yes, the hat."

Just then a young girl approached Lynette. "Is that your dog?" she asked, pointing to Peaches.

"You interrupted me," Lynette scolded the girl. "I was talking."

"But...."

"No buts. You interrupted me, and that was rude."

"But your dog ate my ice cream, and THAT was rude."

Lynette was stumped, but only for a moment.

"I didn't eat your ice cream. The dog did." Not content to let well enough alone, Lynette continued. "Do you have a brother or sister?"

The girl nodded yes.

"Do you like it when you get in trouble for something they've done?"

The girl shook her head no.

"Well, I don't like you blaming me for Peaches eating your ice cream. If you had hung onto it better or held it up higher, she wouldn't have eaten it."

"But dogs aren't allowed on the playground," the girl said pointing to a sign. "You shouldn't have let your dog play there."

"You're blaming me again. She's not my dog." Lynette corrected the girl. "She's my mother's dog."

"Well, then your mom should teach you both better manners!" With that the girl stomped off and headed back to the playground. Lynette was momentarily struck speechless.

"Did you see that?" Lynette turned to Agatha. "I can't believe she talked to me that way, why when I was that age...."

"You were much worse," Agatha said.

Lynette scowled. "You still haven't answered my question. What are you going to do with the hat?"

"Not to be rude," Agatha said, "but why do you want to know?"

"I asked you first," Lynette said.

Agatha didn't see the conversation going anywhere, so she tried to find a way out. "It's been nice chatting with you, but I've got to fix M. Poirot's dinner."

"But it's not even lunchtime, yet!" Lynette argued.

"Tell that to M. Poirot" Agatha said. Then she secured him in the basket, hopped on her bike, and pedaled off.

"Hey," Lynette yelled as she minced along in the wake of Agatha's departure, "that's not fair. I asked you a question!"

Agatha was ready to leave the park and go home. She could picture the immediate future—M. Poirot with his nose in the air busy sniffing the familiar smells of the route home, she with a vision of a much needed revelation for the hat design project.

But no sooner had she escaped Lynette's line of sight than her reverie was interrupted.

CHAPTER SEVEN

Agatha Turns Sleuth

W HILE AGATHA WAS manifesting a completed hat design that would be wildly successful, her bicycle chain slipped from the sprocket. Instead of pedaling toward a new life, she was stuck in the park with no tools and a hungry dog. Drat, she thought, as she got off her bike and pushed it to a spot where the long shadow of a hedge offered respite from the sun. Then she took M. Poirot out of the basket.

With her foot firmly on the handle of his leash, she tried to get the chain back on her bicycle. Then she heard a familiar voice.

"I know he told me to get the hat, mother."

It was Lynette.

Agatha and M. Poirot peaked through the bushes to look.

Lynette held her phone with one hand and kept a firm grip on Peaches's leash with the other.

"I tried to talk to her about it. She said I was rude!"

"Of course I wasn't! Why do you think everything is my fault?"

"I spent over an hour chatting up Angela, and I got nowhere."

"What do you mean, 'who's Angela?' The new QGARST director, of course."

"I thought her name was Angela."

"Why didn't she tell me her name is Andrea?"

"Why would I call her Angela if she had her name tag on?"

"She must not have been wearing it. We should file a complaint!"

"No, I didn't buy anything."

"Much."

"One pair of shoes. That's all."

Since Agatha and M. Poirot had last seen Lynette she had swapped out her pink patent leather dog walking heels for a different pair of equally impractical shoes, presumably the ones she purchased from QGARST just an hour earlier. While she talked with her mother she held out her feet and admired her latest purchase—a pair of open-toed green suede sandals with ankle ties and red and green seaweed-like decorative clumps secured to the toe straps. Lynette was so taken with the shoes, she failed to hear her mother's next question.

"Sure."

"What do you mean what do I mean?"

"I *was* listening," Lynette said defiantly, "but Peaches won't stop whining."

Agatha wished Lynette and her mother would get back to the part of the conversation about the hat.

"I can't pay more attention to her. I'm talking to you!"

"Besides, she was a bad dog," Lynette said.

"She stole a little girl's ice cream. She was so rude."

"What do you mean Peaches is lactose intolerant?"

"You think she's crying because she has a stomachache?"

"What do you mean daddy says I can't come home until I have the hat? Angela—I mean, Andrea—said the hat is Agatha's now, and there's no recourse. She cited some law she said daddy should know."

"Honestly I don't understand why he's fixated on that hat. The horsehair is faded, the colors of the ribbons don't coordinate," Lynette continued, "and the stitching makes it look too busy."

"How does he even know Sevilla made it?"

Agatha and M. Poirot's ears perked up when they heard the now familiar name.

"So what? No one will ever know if we don't tell them."

Lynette had just confirmed Eleanor's account of who made the hat. With this new clue, Agatha had a clear idea what direction the investigation should take, but she needed to get the chain back on her bicycle and get herself and M. Poirot out of the bushes before she could follow up.

Then Peaches came to their rescue. Her whining turned to crying, and Lynette was forced to get off the phone and leave the park. Just as Agatha was about to give up on ever getting the chain back onto her bicycle, it slipped right on.

"Look at that!" she said aloud to the dog. "We can go home!"

M. Poirot understood the word "home," and he wagged his tail.

As they left the park, Agatha's previous reverie where she "manifested" her successful future was replace with a laser-like focus on the past.

From what she heard Lynette say to her mother, the Baileys knew Amelia had a living relation. But, like Agatha, they didn't know who.

"It's encouraging to know they haven't been able to bury the information," Agatha told M. Poirot, "but if a living relation is going to be found so the terms of the will can be exercised, we have no time to waste."

Solving the case would accomplish two important goals. One, it would make a difference in the lives of the rescue animals of Madison County, and two, it would give Agatha enough money to tide her over until she got paid for the crochet hat design.

When they got home Agatha made a much awaited midday meal for M. Poirot and started a pot of coffee for herself. While she waited for the coffee to brew, she turned her attention to the cloche.

It was pretty much exactly as Lynette had described it: made with now faded horsehair, ribbons that didn't coordinate, and top stitching that made it look busy. She examined the embroidery stitches on the ribbons. At first glance, it looked complicated, but on closer inspection she saw it was just a series of running stitches and French knots. Something about it looked vaguely familiar.

Agatha wondered why the mysterious Sevilla went to such effort to make the hat less attractive. Whatever Sevilla's reasons, Agatha needed to get to work on her own design.

She started by trying to work a treble stitch in a spiral to see what she could learn. What she learned was that her crochet skills were decidedly rudimentary. What made her think she could design a crochet hat anyway?

Discouraged, Agatha trudged up the stairs to her room and grabbed the first Nancy Drew from the shelf. Soon, she fell into the story of *The Clue of the Tapping Heels*. In the space of just eleven pages Nancy and her chums learned to tap in Morse code, found an injured Persian kitten, fed the kitten and themselves courtesy of a Miss Pickwick, found the kitten's owner, and returned it to her. While there were, no doubt, more twists and turns ahead, Agatha went back to her crochet project with renewed optimism.

A long strip of horsehair had been used to make the base of the hat. How hard could it be, she wondered, to crochet a straight strip of yarn?

Then, without warning, M. Poirot jumped up and began barking. When Agatha didn't respond immediately, he scurried to the kitchen door and barked in greater earnest.

"Really, M. Poirot? Right when I'm getting this figured out?"

He ignored her and continued to bark.

"Okay," Agatha said, "let's see what's going on." She opened the front door and stepped onto the porch. Looking one way, then the other, she saw nothing that could have caused the dog's distress. Resigned to the interruption, she stepped back into the house, put the dog on his leash, and the two of them set out on a walk with the terrier leading the way.

M. Poirot was very businesslike once they got to the street. He surveyed the landscape as if he knew exactly what he were looking for but couldn't find it. He continued moving quickly, then stopped dead in his tracks. He put up his nose, cocked his head to the side, and stood as still as a statue. Agatha looked to see if anyone were lurking nearby.

She saw two teenagers race down the street on skateboards, a cyclist turn left from Kansas onto Main, and a man in work clothes walk into The Coffee Shop. Everything looked normal.

Just as Agatha had assured herself everything was as it should be, the couple that had nearly run her down when she was waiting to pull out of the cemetery emerged from the hardware store. They appeared to be looking over a purchase, but she could not make out what it was. Then Agatha decided that since she and M. Poirot were out, they should stop by Marcus Hill's office so she could run a few ideas past him.

*   *   *

"What brings the two of you to this end of Grand Avenue?" Marcus greeted them.

"I may have made progress in the case of Amelia Dettmer," Agatha said with a confidence she wasn't certain was warranted.

"Good. I'm due in court on Friday, and if I don't have progress to report to Judge Atkins, she's liable to bite my head off."

"I overheard Lynette talking on the phone with her mother at the park. It seems they think the hat I bought at QGARST the other day is a clue toward finding a relation of Amelia's. I have no idea what kind of clue, but I'm going to go visit Eleanor again to figure out if the hat I have is, in fact, the hat in the photo I saw on her piano."

Marcus had only been half listening to Agatha as he read over a motion on his desk, "Why do think the hat is a clue?"

"I think it's a clue because Lynette's father is so insistent that Lynette get the hat back. There must be something there. I just need to figure out what."

"Be careful, Agatha," Marcus warned. "When the Baileys get it in their heads to do something, they can be very obstinate. It's not always a bad quality, but most of the time it is."

"Don't worry, Marcus, I've got M. Poirot to protect me."

CHAPTER EIGHT

A Discouraging Day

AGATHA COULD TELL Marcus was not convinced that the mysterious Sevilla held the key to solving the Dettmer case. She left his office with M. Poirot in tow. "We'll show him!" she said to the dog once they were outside.

The next day, Agatha packed up the gear she and M. Poirot would need for their investigation and left a note for Mildred telling her they would be home for dinner.

"After our last cemetery excursion, I don't want to get caught in another thunderstorm," she said to the terrier as she surveyed the sky. Then Agatha shook her head. Here she was just a few weeks into her forced retirement, and she was already talking to M. Poirot like he was an operative with The Agency.

She looked out the front window and saw a few wispy clouds, but nothing that looked like rain. Then she pulled up the day's weather cast on her computer. She and M. Poirot watched intently. According to the metro area's most respected meteorologist, the fair weather would continue for another thirty-six hours—more than enough time for them to get to the cemetery and back.

Agatha pedaled swiftly while M. Poirot, perched in his basket like a figurehead on the prow of a sailing ship, enjoyed the twists and turns of the road and the wind in his hair. In no time, they reached the cemetery.

This time when Agatha pulled her bike up onto the gazebo she noticed that it looked more worn than she remembered. It needed a thorough sanding and a fresh coat of paint. As she and M. Poirot took refuge in the shade it provided, Agatha reviewed her plans.

When she was finally ready to investigate, she secured M. Poirot's leash to his collar and the two of them walked over to a stone memorial with the name PLUM in letters that looked to be a foot high. Agatha was certain this was where she had run across the grave of the forgotten Dettmer while trying to catch M. Poirot.

She found the Newmans, she found the Hills, but where was that Dettmer grave? Agatha scoured the area. Had she imagined the whole thing?

Then she heard a bell. The kind that goes off when a car door is left open with the key in the ignition. Agatha turned to look. A young man got out of a truck and walked toward her.

M. Poirot strained at the end of his leash and barked as the man neared.

"Hey, pup." The young man stopped a respectable distance away and looked at M. Poirot with a bemused smile. "Don't you remember me?" He turned to Agatha. "Can I help you?"

He sounded older and more stern than he looked. Agatha had pegged him at a mature seventeen. On closer inspection, he looked to be in his mid-twenties.

"I don't know." Agatha said. "Who are you?"

"Michael Chavez," he said. "Who are you?"

Agatha was now acutely aware she was out in the middle of nowhere with only an ill-tempered 12-pound dog for protection. "Why do you need to know?"

"So when I call Sheriff Georgia Holtz, I can tell her the name of the woman standing at the scene of a crime with a dog that doesn't belong to her," he said. "I've got her number on speed dial."

"Georgia Holtz is the sheriff?" Lydia was right, things had changed.

A lot.

Georgia was named for her grandfather, George, who served as Madison County's 39th sheriff. Because of the popularity of alphabetical order seating, she and Steven Hughes always sat next to each other. They became fast friends in elementary school and spent recess writing up other students for offenses real and imagined.

"Yes," Michael said, "and don't think that because you're a woman she is going to let you off. She's a by-the-book kind of law enforcement officer and running around with a dog that doesn't belong to you isn't going to score points with her," he said matter-of-factly.

"My name is Agatha," she finally said. "Agatha Bigelow, and I didn't steal the dog. He belongs to my mother."

"Nice try, whoever, you are, but I know Mrs. Bigelow personally, and her daughter doesn't live in Quercus Grove. She lives in Istanbul or something, and she sells yarn." He took his phone out and made a call.

"Hey, Aunt Georgia, I think I found the headstone thief."

Headstone thief? Maybe Agatha was in the right place after all. But why would someone steal a headstone? She strained to hear what was being said, but the connection was poor. Georgia's voice was breaking up, and Agatha couldn't make out all the words.

Michael looked at Agatha with renewed suspicion.

"Because she's standing right where the headstone was."

Michael's phone yelled at him.

"She said her name is Agatha Bigelow, but I'm sure she's lying."

Michael's phone yelled at him again.

"Why would Agatha Bigelow be out here? Everyone knows her father is buried at Woodlawn Cemetery."

The phone yelled even louder.

"They never found a body?" Michael looked at Agatha, incredulous at the details his aunt was sharing.

Agatha could have told Michael it never paid to argue with Georgia, but as he went on about whether or not Agatha was Agatha Bigelow, that awful summer her father disappeared came back to her, and her mind replayed the last normal thing she had done before the world she knew was turned upside down.

*   *   *

"I don't want saddle shoes," Agatha said, "I want those!" She pointed to a pair of shiny brown penny loafers in the window of the shoe store.

"Agatha, we already talked about this," her mother sighed.

"No," Agatha said, "you talked about it. I just had to listen."

Her mother hesitated. "I'll make you a deal. You can have the black and white saddle shoes instead of the brown and white."

"But I don't want saddle shoes! I want penny loafers!" Agatha crossed her arms.

After some back and forth, Agatha agreed to try them on. She was certain that this late in August the local shoe store wouldn't have black and white saddle shoes in her size, and then her mother would be forced to choose between driving to the quad cities metro area or getting Agatha the penny loafers.

"I'm sorry," Mr. Roberts said as he emerged from a room in the back of the store where the shoes were kept, "we don't have the black and white saddle shoes in your size, Agatha. But you're in luck! We have one last pair of the brown and white saddle shoes that should fit. They're very popular," he added.

Popular schmopular, Agatha thought. Grown-ups, she noticed, were really big on the truth until they had to tell it.

"Let's try them on," he said, pulling a shoehorn from his back pocket.

To Agatha's dismay the shoes fit perfectly. Her dream of a pair of shiny penny loafers complete with a lucky penny were dashed. She was going to have to make do with her last choice — again — a pair of brown and white saddle shoes.

Her mother tried to mollify her with a pair of white ruffled pink bobby socks.

It didn't work.

* * *

"I was already out this way and thought I would pull into the cemetery to see if there were any clues your deputies overlooked. That's when I saw her ride in on a bicycle. Can't miss it. It's bright orange and has a basket on the front, and she's got Mrs. Bigelow's dog!"

Michael cast his eyes back at Agatha.

"You're sure?"

Finally, Michael's phone yelled loud enough for Agatha to hear.

"If I say it's Agatha Bigelow, it's Agatha Bigelow!"

That was the Georgia Agatha knew.

Michael ended the call and looked at her warily.

"My aunt says you are Agatha Bigelow, but you still haven't explained why you're right on top of the spot where the Dettmer headstone used to be!"

Agatha wasn't happy to be interrogated, but now she had confirmation that there had been a Dettmer headstone right where she was standing, and she had not imagined the whole thing. Meanwhile, M. Poirot took exception to Michael's tone and growled in disapproval. While Agatha agreed with M. Poirot's assessment, she didn't think growling at Michael would help, so she tried logic.

"If I took the headstone," Agatha said, "why would I need to come out to the cemetery?"

Michael rubbed his chin while he thought about what she said.

"Besides, I couldn't fit a headstone into this basket," Agatha continued. "Whoever took it, has to have a car."

"Maybe," Michael conceded. "But I'm going to keep an eye on you."

Despite his aunt's lecture, Agatha could tell he still regarded her as the prime suspect in the theft.

She took one last look at the patch of dirt where the Dettmer headstone had been. It seemed to have disappeared into thin air, just as Agatha's father had.

*   *   *

One day Agatha had a father just like every other kid she knew, and the next day he was gone.

"Presumed dead," was what the men who came to the door told her mother.

Agatha should have been asleep, but instead she was under the covers reading *The Mystery of the 99 Steps*. She had just gotten to the part where Monsieur Leblanc was walking into the study to answer the telephone when there was a knock at the front door of the Bigelow house.

Soon, Agatha heard her mother's voice call out, "Coming!"

As Lydia Bigelow made her way to the door, Agatha came out of her room and stood at the top of the stairs where she was invisible in the shadows.

"Mrs. Bigelow?"

"Yes," Agatha's mother said.

"Sorry to disturb you. I'm Mr. Dixon, and this is my partner, Mr. Hicks," said one of the men.

"Do you have identification?" Lydia asked.

The men each pulled out a billfold and showed Agatha's mother their IDs.

"Why are you here?" she finally said.

"We regret to inform you," Mr. Dixon began, "that your husband, Ralph Bigelow, fell overboard and has been missing for twelve hours. The search will resume in the morning. At this point he is presumed dead."

Overboard? Agatha thought her father was on a business trip. He sold farm equipment. Why would he be on a boat?

"Do you have any questions?" Mr. Dixon asked.

"Has his briefcase been found?" Lydia said.

"I don't know, but I can look into that for you," Mr. Dixon said.

Lydia took in a sharp breath and squared her shoulders. "Thank you," she said and slowly closed the door.

*　　*　　*

Agatha watched Michael walk back to his truck. He got in, pretended to adjust the mirror, then shut the door. After her brush with the nephew of the law, she figured she had learned all she could about the headstone and decided to go see Eleanor. Maybe she would know something.

After a short ride, Agatha turned into the driveway and pulled her bike up to the back door that led to the mudroom. She knocked at the door, but there was no answer. She looked in the window, and was surprised to find Oscar looking back at her. She waved at the cat, then she and M. Poirot resumed the search for Eleanor.

The first time Agatha had come to the farmhouse she had been running across a field in the rain while chasing after M. Poirot and trying not to get hit by lightning. There were a few things she had missed as a result of the weather and her duress at the dog's escape.

The house, which had looked inviting when they had arrived in a downpour, looked more foreboding and less well kept in the glare of the sunlight. There were dried ruts in the driveway and the gravel was sparse in the more trafficked areas. The windows and the trim looked like they could use a fresh coat of paint, as did the barn.

Agatha was about to give up and go home when a truck pulled into the driveway. It was Eleanor. After parking next to the barn, she emerged with a bag of cat food.

"Why hello, M. Poirot," Eleanor greeted the terrier, "I hope you weren't waiting long," she reached down to scratch him behind his ears. "I had to go into town to get Oscar his prescription cat food," she explained to the dog. "It's awfully good to see you! And you, too," she said, finally acknowledging Agatha. "I hope you have time to come in. I have a crochet piece I want to show you."

Amused M. Poirot merited a warmer greeting than she did, Agatha was delighted to have an invitation to come in. Now she would not need to create a pretext. She had learned the hard way that in life—as in spying—it was easier if you were able to stick to the truth.

She didn't know if honesty was always the best policy, but it was easier to remember and getting caught in a lie had its own perils.

"I found this after you left the other day." Agatha looked at the piece in Eleanor's hands and saw that it was a Bruges crochet doily. "I hate for it to sit on my dresser without an audience to appreciate it. I'm hoping that in your new career as a crochet designer, you'll find a use for it."

Agatha held the doily in her hands and examined it. "This is beautiful work," she said. "It really should be in a museum."

"Museum, schmuseum," Eleanor said. "It needs to be updated and brought into the 21st century so it doesn't die off completely. I don't mean for you to start crocheting with thread, but I do think this pattern is worth preserving, and...." Eleanor stopped mid-sentence.

"And," Agatha prompted her, hoping the older woman hadn't lost her thought.

"And?" Eleanor said looking puzzled for a moment. Then her face gave away that she remembered what she was going to say but had decided not to. "Nothing, nothing at all."

The way she said "nothing" rang hollow. Agatha wondered what was on her mind and tried to use M. Poirot to get the truth out of her.

"M. Poirot wants to know what you were going to say," Agatha offered. "Look he's waiting for you to finish." She pointed to M. Poirot with his head cocked to one side and looking at Eleanor as if he were waiting to hear the end of her sentence.

"I don't mean to be unkind, Agatha, but that's nonsense. He wants chicken and rice, don't you M. Poirot?" she said turning to him as she walked toward the kitchen. He barked in agreement.

Eleanor pulled out a bowl of rice from the refrigerator and a sandwich bag of what looked like yellow ice cubes from the freezer. "I make chicken broth," she explained, "and freeze it in ice cube trays. Then I have perfect pet portions I can thaw them in the microwave whenever there is a snack emergency. Annie loved chicken broth. I do miss her so."

"She must have been quite a dog."

"Oh, she was." Eleanor got a far away look in her eye.

"That reminds me, I have a question for you." Agatha reached into her bag. "I bought this hat the other day at QGARST. I thought it looked a lot like the one in that photo on your piano."

Eleanor took the cloche in her hands to examine it. "It certainly does," her features sharpened, and she looked as if she were trying to hide her true expression. "You say you bought this at QGARST?"

"Yes," Agatha paused to assess Eleanor's response, "It seems Mrs. Bailey donated it, and then sent her daughter Lynette to get it back. By then, I had already purchased it, so it's mine now," Agatha said with a small smile.

"Good for you," Eleanor said.

The microwave dinged. "And now, M. Poirot gets his reward for being such a good dog," Eleanor said triumphantly.

"As for the hat," Eleanor said, "if there's anyone alive who knows the story behind it, it's Abigail Rowen. She lives at the Quercus Grove Assisted Living Center on the third floor. Take this photo," Eleanor said thrusting it into Agatha's hands. "It might help jog her memory."

CHAPTER NINE

Vital Information

O N THE RIDE home Eleanor's words rang in Agatha's ears. The more she thought about it, the more she realized she needed to talk to Abigail Rowen.

Now.

Abigail wasn't getting any younger, and neither was Agatha. And who knew what the Baileys would do? It was clear they were trying to sweep something under the rug.

Agatha needed to find out what.

There was just one problem. What would she do with M. Poirot?

When they got home, Agatha went straight to the phone.

"Law offices of Marcus Hill, how may I direct your call?"

"Claudia?"

"No, this is the answering service. Claudia and Mr. Hill will be in court until four o'clock. Do you want to leave a message?"

"Ask Claudia to call Agatha Bigelow," Agatha said.

"Will do!" the answering service operator said chirpily.

She tried the next number she had.

"Camp Bow Wow. This is Mariah, how can I help you?"

"Can I bring my mom's dog in for a half day?"

"Sure. What's your mom's dog's name?"

"M. Poirot."

"Oh." There was a long pause. "Unfortunately, he's only allowed to come when Danielle is here, and she's out on maternity leave. She'll be back in four weeks. Do you want me to put him down for a play date when she returns?"

"No thank you," Agatha said with a sigh.

"Okay. Thanks for making Camp Bow Wow your doggy day care of choice!"

After just two calls Agatha had run through her options, There was only one thing left to do: organize a reconnaissance mission that included M. Poirot.

"Operation Abigail, it is!" she said.

Agatha crafted a cover story as she assembled their props—a notebook with an official looking seal, an equally official looking bag filled with dog treats, the photo Eleanor gave her, and the hat.

Less than half an hour later, they pulled up to Quercus Grove Assisted Living Center. As she locked her bike Agatha went over the details of their cover story one half-truth at a time.

"So you're a therapy dog!" She explained, hoping her enthusiasm would impress upon M. Poirot the importance of the work they were undertaking.

Then she glanced at her reflection in the large glass doors before they automatically slid open. With her official looking bag slung over one shoulder and M. Poirot in tow, she thought she looked like she could be a therapy animal paraprofessional.

"I'm here to see Abigail Rowen," Agatha said to the young man at the reception desk. This was true.

"You'll need to sign in, but you can't bring your dog," he said without looking up from his phone.

"He's not my dog." Also true.

The young man continued scrolling. "You still can't bring him in."

"He's a therapy dog." This was a half-truth. M. Poirot was, after all, a dog.

"I'll need to see the order so I can enter it in the log book."

"No one gave me an order," she said. This was very true.

"If you were a friend of the family and this were your therapy dog, it would not violate any policies," he said offering her a way around the rule.

"But I don't have his therapy dog certificate with me," she said.

"If he's your therapy dog, I can't ask for the certificate. Then there are only two requirements. You need to be a friend of the family, and," he said, "you need to sign in."

Agatha knew from reading the pioneers applications in search of clues for a living relation to Amelia Dettmer that the Rowens, like the Bigelows, were Pioneers of Quercus Grove. So it stood to reason they must have been friends at some point in the past 150 years. Agatha signed the log book with a clear conscience.

"Where is Mrs. Rowen's room?" she asked.

"Third floor. Elevators are over there," the receptionist said pointing to a long hall.

"What's her room number?"

"A nurse will help you when you get there," he said turning back to his phone.

Agatha pushed the button for the elevator. M. Poirot, sat at her feet and waited patiently. While not a therapy dog, he was proving to be an able spy. She rehearsed their cover story one last time while they waited. It took forever, but eventually the elevator doors opened and revealed floor to ceiling mirrors with ornate red and gold carpet on the floor.

They stepped in, and she pushed the button for the third floor. After a slight hesitation, the elevator began its ascent. Agatha was aware of every creak as she ruminated on their situation thinking of all the ways it could go wrong. Meanwhile, M. Poirot was too busy trying to engage the dog in the mirror to notice her discomfort. Finally the doors of the elevator opened, and the two agents of "Operation Abigail" stepped out into the third-floor lobby where they were greeted by a nurse.

"Can I help you?" he said in a friendly but businesslike tone.

"I'm here to see Abigail Rowen," Agatha said.

"I'll need you to sign in. Then I can show you to her room," he said.

Agatha could see they took security seriously here. She never would have been able to do her work for The Agency if yarn shops had sign in systems like the one at this assisted living facility.

M. Poirot took a shine to the nurse and did his best to get his attention, first sitting quietly and then offering a paw.

"Who is this?" the nurse asked. M. Poirot wagged his tail, happy to have caught the nurse's attention.

"M. Poirot," Agatha said. She almost forgot they were on a reconnaissance mission and was about to explain he was her mother's dog. Thankfully, she stopped herself before she blew her cover. "He's a therapy dog. I get a bit claustrophobic in closed spaces," she said.

The nurse bent down to shake the paw M. Poirot had proffered. "He is certainly charming and well behaved. Some of our visitors could learn a thing or two from him," the nurse said as if he had someone in mind.

Then, with a wave of his hand, he signaled for Agatha and M. Poirot to follow him.

They went down one hall, turned left, then walked to the end of another long hall where the nurse stopped in front of a bright pink door. Next to the door was a shadow box with memorabilia that included the senior portrait of a young woman, a post card of Paris, and a letter signed *Sincerely, Sevilla.*

Agatha's heart quickened at the sight of the now familiar name.

Abigail was dozing in a reclining chair.

"Miss Abigail, you have visitors," the nurse said. "Miss Abigail," he repeated gently. Her eyes fluttered open. "A Miss Bigelow is here to see you."

Abigail stared right through Agatha for a very long moment, then shook off her slumber.

"I'll leave you to visit," the nurse said, then left the room as quickly and quietly as he had brought them to it.

"Who are you?" Abigail's tone conveyed interest and suspicion.

"Agatha Bigelow. My father was Ralph Bigelow." A flicker of recognition crossed the older woman's face.

"Ah, yes, Ralph. Married an out-of-towner as I recall." She reached down to pet M. Poirot, "What's this little guy's name?" Abigail asked, more interested in the dog than Agatha.

"M. Poirot," Agatha said. "He's named after...."

"The detective in *Murder on the Orient Express*." Abigail turned to the dog. "M. Poirot, to what do I owe this visit from a world famous detective? Are you here to solve a crime?"

M. Poirot offered no reply other than to sidle up to her so she could scratch behind his ears and rub under his chin.

"You have an interesting shadow box" Agatha said.

Abigail didn't acknowledge Agatha's statement and instead proceeded with questions of her own.

"What did you say his name was?" the older woman asked.

"M. Poirot," Agatha replied.

"And what did you say your name was?" she asked.

"Agatha Bigelow."

"And your father's name is Ralph?"

"Yes," Agatha said.

Abigail's eyes narrowed, "isn't your name Agatha Christine?"

"It is," she said.

"Are you any relation to Agatha Christie the writer?" the older woman asked.

"No," Agatha said.

"But your dog's name is M. Poirot."

Agatha started to say it was her mother's dog, but stopped before the words left her mouth. "Yes, and I've thought if I ever got a cat, I would like to name her Miss Marple."

The part about the cat was true. For as long as Agatha could remember, she had wanted one.

"So why did you come to see me?" Abigail asked.

"I'm so glad you asked! I saw this picture at Eleanor Frickenstein's house, and she said you might know the story of the hat that Amelia is wearing," Agatha said pulling the photo out of her bag to show the older woman.

"So I do," Abigail looked out the nearby window. "Does Eleanor still live out on that farm next to the haunted cemetery?"

"She does," Agatha said. Then she pulled the cloche out of her bag hoping to keep the conversation on topic. "Is this the hat in the photo?"

Abigail's gaze moved from the window to M. Poirot. "I don't know." Then she looked at Agatha. "He's a very good dog."

"He is." Maybe, Agatha thought, she should try flattery. "Eleanor said if anyone would know about this hat, it was Abigail Rowen!"

"I suppose, but I'd rather visit with your dog." The older woman focused her attention on M. Poirot, and he, in return, focused his attention on her. Feeling a bit like an uninvited guest, Agatha looked out the window that Abigail had looked out earlier, and she spied the now familiar burgundy car pulling into the parking lot.

"Where's the hat?" Abigail asked abruptly.

"Oh, the hat." Agatha was looking at the mysterious car that now straddled four parking spaces.

She fumbled trying to find the cloche. "It's right here," she said as she plucked it from the end table next to Abigail's chair and placed it on the older woman's lap.

Abigail picked up the cloche and turned it over in her hands. "Sevilla told me all about this hat."

Agatha was trying to pay attention to Abigail and keep an eye on the burgundy sedan. "Is there a story to it?"

"There's a story to everything," Abigail said. "Do you know what this is made of?"

"The woman who sold it to me said it was genuine horsehair," Agatha said, trying to watch the couple as they got out of the car then walked out of view.

"The woman who sold it to you was right."

With the couple completely out of sight, Agatha gave Abigail her full attention.

"Can you tell me anything about the ribbons?" But Agatha wasn't quick enough. Abigail's focus was no longer on the hat.

"Look at the people out there," the older woman said pointing to the window.

"What people?" Agatha asked, her eyes following the direction of Abigail's finger.

It was the couple from the burgundy car. They were already back from wherever they had gone to.

"They were stealing the roses!" Abigail said.

Agatha stood up and walked to the window. She didn't see any roses to steal and wondered how the older woman could have seen the couple from where she sat. Before she could say anything, Abigail continued her story.

"The other day my niece took me to St. James Cemetery—it was the day we had that dreadful thunderstorm—and that woman took the roses right off Amelia Dettmer's grave. I know trouble when I see it, and those two are up to no good!"

Agatha knew Abigail was right about the couple being up to no good, but she found it hard to believe that they went to St. James Cemetery to steal cut roses. What value could there be in nearly dead flowers?

No, Agatha told herself. I have two tasks to complete: The first is to figure out who Amelia's living relation is, and the second is to design a crochet hat. I don't need another mystery to solve.

"What can you tell me about this stitching on the hat?" Agatha asked.

"I can't tell you anything." Abigail made a motion as if she were zipping her lips closed, then she reached down to pet the dog.

"Why can't you tell me?" Agatha asked.

"Because it's a secret!" Abigail said with a smile, "and if I told you, it wouldn't be a secret. You know," the older woman paused uncertain if she should continue. "Amelia Dettmer knew the Baileys' secret." Then she whispered as if to make sure no one else could hear, "Amelia knew everybody's secrets."

CHAPTER TEN

Abigail's Disclosure

A GATHA HELD HER breath and waited.

After a long silence, Abigail finally spoke. "You know," she said, "Sevilla wasn't just a famous hat maker, she was also a spy."

A spy? In Quercus Grove? Unbelievable. But where would Abigail have gotten such an idea if it weren't true? If it were true, who would Sevilla have been spying for? And what about the secrets Abigail insisted Amelia was keeping? Had they died with her, or was this peculiar term in her will Amelia's way of revealing her secrets from the grave?

Agatha nudged M. Poirot closer to Abigail hoping his presence would persuade her to elaborate on both Sevilla's career as a spy and the Baileys' secret.

"He's so sweet." Abigail paused. "Where were we?"

With one eye on Abigail, and one eye on the window, Agatha watched the couple in the burgundy car drive away. "You were telling me that Amelia Dettmer knew everybody's secrets."

"Yes, she did. She even knew the secret of that hat. Something to do with a coded message. Just like a spy novel."

Agatha spent the first eighteen years of her life in Quercus Grove, and she never encountered anything interesting enough to be the plot for a Nancy Drew book, let alone a spy novel.

She hoped Abigail would tell her more about the secrets.

"They should have told the truth," Abigail finally declared, "but they thought it would ruin them." She turned to Agatha, "I will never understand people who think hiding the truth is acceptable."

The meeting with Abigail was getting stranger and stranger.

"What was the message?" Agatha asked.

"The message?"

"The coded message in the hat," Agatha reminded her.

Abigail smiled like the Cheshire Cat. "I can't tell you that. If I do, it will spoil the secret."

And if Agatha didn't find out what that secret was, it would spoil things for the many rescue animals of Madison County that Amelia had taken in. Agatha was out of ideas about how to pry the truth locked inside Abigail's brain in the "circa 1930s" section, but at least now she knew what she was looking for.

Sort of.

"How did you know I like dogs?" Abigail asked.

"Everyone likes M. Poirot," Agatha lied. She wondered how much longer M. Poirot could behave.

"You know, Mrs. Bailey grows beautiful roses," Abigail said. Then with a conspiratorial air the older woman confided,

"She's not really a Bailey of course because she married into the family, but she led her husband to believe she was an Atherton. But she wasn't. She was a Kelly. Why she wasn't even born in this state let alone this county! Can you imagine? Back then the Baileys were the *crème de la crème* of Quercus Grove, and they have deep, deep roots in Madison County. I can't imagine how betrayed Mr. Bailey must have felt when he realized he'd been hoodwinked."

Hoodwinked? Agatha wanted to steer the conversation back to spies and secrets and codes. "Maybe love does conquer all. I mean, they did have Lynette," Agatha said.

"Did you ever wonder why they just had one child?" Abigail asked. "I'll tell you," then she answered her own question. "When Mr. Bailey found out about his wife's deception, it was too late! They were already married and had a child! To divorce her would have brought nothing but shame. But if the truth got out, it might ruin him completely!"

What truth could have gotten out that could cause Mr. Bailey's ruin? And how did this relate to Sevilla? Agatha thought Abigail's description had to be hyperbole. Lynette was born in the 20th century for goodness sake. Who would care if Mr. Bailey had married a Pioneer of Quercus Grove? But Agatha had learned the hard way assumptions could be hazardous to your health. "How would it ruin him?" she asked.

"I shouldn't tell you," Abigail said, shaking her head. "I really shouldn't."

Agatha was now more curious.

"Have you ever wondered," Abigail finally said in a very pointed way, "why Lynette Bailey has never held a job?"

Agatha left Quercus Grove for college more than 30 years earlier and only came back for brief visits on holidays. She didn't know Lynette hadn't had a job. Now that she was back in town, she knew that Lynette's nails and hair were always perfect, and even though she had become quite the thrifter in the wake of Quercus Grove's "sparks joy" campaign, she still spent money on salons, coffee shops, and pricey high-heel shoes. She was getting money from somewhere.

In all of her errand running and sleuthing on the roads of Madison County and all through Quercus Grove since she returned, Agatha hadn't seen Lynette's face on any billboards asking "Have you seen this bank robber?" However Lynette got her money, it must at least *seem* legal.

"Maybe her dad gives her an allowance?" Agatha said, even though that sounded ridiculous.

"And where do you think he gets the money for her allowance?" Abigail asked.

"From his work?" Agatha didn't even know if Lynette got an allowance. She didn't know where this conversation was headed and hoped Abigail would tell her.

"Pfft," Abigail snorted.

Agatha waited for the older woman to finish, but as far as Abigail was concerned, she had laid out everything needed to solve the case. It was like having one piece of a tantalizing 500-piece puzzle without the other 499 pieces and no idea where to look for them. Agatha was sure that Amelia Dettmer had something on the Baileys, but what? And if Abigail's memories were correct, it was a small part of a much larger puzzle.

Who, Agatha wondered, was the missing relation? And was that person connected to Sevilla? More importantly what would it mean for Quercus Grove if and when Agatha uncovered the truth? Or more to the point, what would it mean to Quercus Grove if Agatha did not uncover the truth?

The day was not turning out as Agatha hoped. She came to see Abigail in search of answers, but every answer she got came with five more questions. She still didn't know who Sevilla was, what the secret code in the hat was, or where the code might be. And M. Poirot, while enchanted by Abigail, was going to want to eat soon. Agatha needed to wrap up the visit. She tried one last time to find out about Sevilla the milliner turned spy and the code in the hat.

"Can you tell me how this was made?" Agatha asked. The older woman started with what Agatha already knew.

"Sevilla took a long strip of horsehair and worked in a spiral. She told me what she used to connect the strip of horsehair, but I don't remember now," the older woman said.

Agatha scribbled furiously in her notebook recalling as many details of their wide ranging conversation as she could. She wrote notes about the cloche and everything Abigail had shared about spies, codes, and secrets.

Abigail seemed exhausted by the effort it took to speak; she sat back in her chair and closed her eyes. After a few minutes of silence, M. Poirot barked, waking the old woman from her trance like state.

"Lynette's mother has a real talent with roses," Abigail said, seemingly apropos of nothing. "You know, that hat would have looked lovely with roses on it. I don't know why a rose couldn't be the secret message." She looked around the room "Where is the dog?"

M. Poirot heard the word "dog" and was at Abigail's side in a flash.

"Here he is," Abigail smiled, pleased he had come to her. "You know, Amelia started her animal rescue because Sevilla got called away to do more spying. She had a dog she loved very much, but he really wasn't a very lovable dog. Amelia was the only one who would take him in."

"Do you know where Sevilla went?"

"Yes I do," Abigail said slyly.

Agatha hoped the older woman would share her secret, but she didn't.

Abigail would have been an excellent spy. She clearly loved secrets and loved keeping them even more. Agatha had not expected her largest problem to be persuading Abigail to divulge the truths she knew.

"Hand me that book," Abigail directed. Agatha reached a shelf with no more than a dozen volumes on it. This one was titled *Millinery*. "You know, Sevilla studied with her, she said pointing to the name of the author on the cover, Jane Loewen.

"No, I didn't know that."

"At the University of Chicago," Abigail said with obvious pride. "That's where she met her contacts and learned how to spy. Her father wasn't going to let her go, but it turned out she was even more determined to go to school than he was to make her stay home. You know, in those days, it wasn't easy for a woman to get an education. He almost didn't allow her to go to high school. Can you imagine?"

Abigail and Agatha were silent for a moment.

"No," Agatha said, "I can't. So she studied how to make hats at the University of Chicago?"

"Yes, only it was called millinery, because of the hat makers of Milan. They were excellent, and Sevilla studied in Chicago. Very honorable profession. She liked it because she got to use math. It was her favorite subject in school."

"Jane Loewen would say, 'Millinery is an outstanding example of the practical application of geometry.' Sevilla told me Miss Loewen used to say that at almost every class meeting!"

Abigail sighed. The sigh seemed to transport her back to her childhood when she would listen to Sevilla's stories of spying, secret codes, and hat making.

After an almost hour long visit, Agatha and M. Poirot said their good-byes.

"What do you think she meant by 'they should have told the truth?'" Agatha asked the terrier. M. Poirot looked at Agatha as if to say "I have no idea."

Everything Abigail had shared made the thoughts in Agatha's brain feel like a jumbled mess. Just eight weeks ago she would have taken herself out for a coffee somewhere in Istanbul to sort through them. With M. Poirot in tow, and her bank balance barely hovering north of zero, her options were more limited, but she still had one.

M. Poirot wagged his tail and barked with what sounded like joy when Agatha pulled up to QGARST. Mildred's decluttering had picked up steam since Lydia left town, and Agatha and M. Poirot were now regulars. Agatha's room was becoming more spacious one box at a time.

Agatha enjoyed spending time with Andrea and hoped Andrea would have insight into the stories Abigail had shared. It might even help that Andrea was from out-of-town. She would not be shackled with the same beliefs and biases about Quercus Grove that Agatha was.

"Hello, strangers," Andrea greeted them. "I don't think I've seen you in at least three days!" she teased.

"It hasn't been that long, has it?" Agatha said in mock horror. "I was hoping you could help me."

"What a coincidence," Andrea said, "I was hoping you could help me! You go first!"

"I was wondering if—as you've sorted through the items that no longer spark joy in Madison County—you had come across anything about a woman named Sevilla."

"Not that I recall. What was Sevilla's last name?" Andrea asked.

"I don't know," Agatha admitted.

"I can't say that I have, but I have been inundated with donations. It could be that I haven't come across it or that I didn't notice it."

"Okay. You helped me, now how can I help you?" Agatha asked.

"I'm supposed to be in two places at once," Andrea said. "Sam from The Coffee Shop is a very accomplished calligrapher, and she's coming to help me address envelopes for our big fundraiser, but Mrs. Bailey asked me to come to her house and pick up a bag of things she is donating for the silent auction of this same fundraiser. As you know I'm not on the best of terms with the Baileys since the hat debacle. If you could pick it up, I would be so appreciative."

"If you can watch M. Poirot for me, I'll be glad to do it. I need an excuse to get in the Baileys' house and see if I can find any confirmation of what Abigail Rowen told me. If I'm not back in an hour, you'd better call Officer Steven Hughes and ask him to come find me!" Agatha said, as she waved good-bye.

CHAPTER ELEVEN

Visiting the Baileys

WHEN AGATHA LEFT her meeting with Abigail she had wondered how she would get into the Baileys' house without breaking the law. Andrea being doubled booked was a lucky break that provided just the pretext she needed to get her foot in the door. If she could just get into the living room, she might be able to solve the case!

The town clock struck four as Agatha pulled up to the Baileys' house.

It was a stately affair with an impeccably manicured lawn that would have been ideal for croquet if anyone besides the landscaping crew were allowed to set foot on it. The Baileys were house-proud and it showed. There was not a leaf or weed in sight.

Mrs. Bailey was a very active — some complained too active — member of Quercus Grove Master Gardeners. She taught a number of classes on assorted gardening topics and was recognized as the local rose expert.

Agatha parked her bike on the walkway that led to the house. She made her way past a moat of roses and up some steps to a wraparound porch where she was confronted by the face of a sneering lion. The brass door knocker looked out of place and pretentious — not unlike the Baileys — but before she could lift it from its hinge, the door opened and a young woman hurtled toward Agatha. A man's footsteps could be heard coming after her.

"Nicole!" It was Mr. Bailey. "You *have* to stay."

"That's Ms. Oliver to you," the woman said sharply, "and I don't have to do anything I don't want to do."

"How am I going to manage Peaches?" he asked.

"Not my problem," she replied.

"But I have a motion I need to finish and get to the court-house within the hour!"

"Then you'd better hurry up." With that, Ms. Nicole Oliver turned on her heel nearly running into Agatha. "You've got a visitor!" she announced to her now former employer.

Mr. Bailey, his brow furrowed, looked out the door. "It's so difficult to find good help these days." He brightened when he saw Agatha, "but the agency did send a replacement rather quickly. Hopefully you'll work out better than the woman before you," he said holding the door. "Come in and I'll show you around."

"I'm not from the agency," Agatha said once the door shut behind her.

"You're not from the agency?" he said. "But I have a very important motion I need to file in the case of Amelia Dettmer. If you could just watch my wife's dog, Peaches, while I finish this—I could pay you." He pulled a crisp bill from his wallet. "How does ten dollars sound?"

Agatha decided to keep those thoughts to herself. "Andrea Walker sent me to pick up some things your wife wanted to donate to QGARST for the upcoming silent auction."

"You're not from the agency, you're not Andrea Walker," Mr. Bailey said. His brow furrowed again. "Just who are you?"

"I'm Agatha Bigelow."

"Agatha Bigelow?" He paused then his face clouded over. "Oh, Ralph and Lydia's daughter," he said. "Now what did you say you wanted?"

"Mrs. Bailey asked Andrea to come to pick up a donation to QGARST."

"Well, you'll have to wait until my wife gets home," Mr. Bailey said. "I have work to do!" He left Agatha in the foyer and returned to his study.

At least I got into the Baileys' house without breaking the law, Agatha thought.

The foyer was attractive, but impersonal. There was a vase filled with a selection of Mrs. Bailey's famous roses, an oblong mirror, and a small bronze statue of a lion that looked a lot like the door knocker.

Unlike her own childhood home which had knickknacks that documented the life and times of the Bigelows in Madison County from 1840 forward, there was not a single item in the foyer that pointed to the fact that anyone in the house descended from Pioneers of Quercus Grove. Just as Agatha thought it was safe to step into the living room for a peek at what was there, she heard the distinct cadence of Lynette Bailey's footfall coming up the walk.

When Agatha worked for The Agency, she learned to identify contacts by the sound of their walk. She made it a habit to
station herself across from the person most alert to the comings
and goings of others. That person — every yarn shop had at
least one — knew the names of each and every customer, and
would greet each one as they entered the store. This allowed
Agatha to learn the footfall associated with a specific person
while never having to look up from her work. Looking back on
her life, Agatha realized the first footfall she learned to identify
was Lynette's as she walked in late to most of her classes — the
sound, which grew louder as it neared the door — definitely
belonged to Lynette.

"Father!" Lynette yelled as she barreled through the door,
nearly running over Agatha.

"What are you doing here?" she said, clearly annoyed to
find her childhood frenemy in the foyer.

"Andrea Walker sent me to pick up a bag of things your
mother wanted to donate to QGARST. Maybe you know
where it is?"

"No, I don't. Besides," Lynette continued, "I don't have
time for this!"

"FATHER!" Lynette called again.

The door to her father's office opened and he looked out.
"Please use your indoor voice, Lynette," he said.

"This *is* my indoor voice!" she yelled.

"It doesn't sound like an indoor voice," her father said. "If
you spoke like that to Judge Atkins — who, by the way, will be
making the decision on this motion — she would have you in
the county jail for contempt so fast, your head would spin."

Agatha could hear Lynette's eyes roll.

"Hmphf." Lynette said.

"Remember, Lynette, this is about the Bailey legacy in Madison County. We cannot let Amelia Dettmer best us again."

Agatha's ears perked up at the mention of Amelia Dettmer. How had she bested them in life? And more importantly, how could she best them from the grave?

Agatha was so busy trying to eavesdrop on the conversation, she almost missed the sound of Mrs. Bailey's footsteps.

"Agatha?" Mrs. Bailey said at the unpleasant surprise.

"Yes, Mrs. Bailey, Andrea Walker asked me to...." They were interrupted by the clatter of Peaches running to greet her mistress. The dog came to an abrupt stop when she saw Agatha then barked.

"Use your indoor voice, Peaches" Mrs. Bailey said. "We have company, so you must be polite," but before she could get her dog settled down, Lynette burst out of her father's office.

"Your dog!" Lynette said loudly, "has made a mess of everything!"

"Peaches is not 'my dog,'" her mother said firmly. "She is a valued member of the family, and you are to treat her with the respect she deserves."

"But...."

"No buts," she said sharply.

"But I have to clean up the mess she made. It isn't fair!"

"Life isn't fair." Mrs. Bailey said coolly, her eyes narrowing.

After Lynette's outburst, Mrs. Bailey set her purse on the foyer table and tried to soothe the dog. "You're a good girl," she cooed, "yes you are." With Peaches settled, she finally spoke to Agatha, "Now what were you saying?"

"Andrea sent me to pick up a donation for the silent auction."

"Oh that," Mrs. Bailey said. Then, with a motion of her hand, she directed Agatha to another room.

"This way," Mrs. Bailey said briskly. "You can sit here while I get the donation," she said pointing to a sofa. Then she left the room with Peaches trailing after her.

Agatha took her assigned seat and discovered she had been ordered to wait in the very room she wanted to examine. From where she sat she could see everything. At first, nothing stood out, but just as Mrs. Bailey's footsteps could be heard returning to the living room, Agatha spied a photo on the end table next to the sofa where she was sitting. And it wasn't just any photo. It was the same photo on Eleanor Frickenstein's piano.

"Here." Mrs. Bailey handed Agatha a bag filled with thread crochet. "I don't know what people are supposed to do with these sorts of things nowadays. Doilies aren't much good for anything but collecting dust!"

"Did you know," Agatha began as she tried to sneak another peak at the photo, "doilies are named for a dry goods merchant by the name of Mr. Doyley who lived in sixteenth century London?"

Mrs. Bailey's frown deepened.

Agatha's enthusiasm, however, was undimmed, and she dove into the bag. "Look at this!" she said pulling a piece of filet crochet from the depths of the bag.

Mrs. Bailey scowled. "What am I supposed to see?"

"The rose motif," Agatha said, tracing a finger along the edge of the design. "Don't you want to keep it?"

Mrs. Bailey snatched the doily from Agatha's hand to study it.

"I couldn't help but notice that it looks like those lovely roses you have alongside your front porch." Agatha said.

"You like them?" Mrs. Bailey asked.

"I do," Agatha said, "and the scent is heavenly!"

"It's a new rose I'm cultivating," Mrs. Bailey said. "I've been working on it for years, and it's almost ready to be brought to market. With the right promotion and a little luck my rose will be known all over the world!" In an instant, her face was transformed from annoyance to exuberance. She turned her attention back to the doily. "I can't believe how many times I've walked right past this and never noticed the rose. Funny how we can miss what is right in front of us."

Just like that photo, Agatha thought. "Does that mean you want to keep it?"

"Heavens, no!" Mrs. Bailey replied. "I don't have time for doilies."

Agatha left the Baileys' excited to have finally made progress, but before she could give the odd, albeit successful, mission more thought, the mysterious couple in the burgundy car drove past.

She hopped on her bike and went after them in hot pursuit.

CHAPTER TWELVE

Following a Clue

A GATHA CHASED THE burgundy car pedaling as fast as she could. She was about to turn left onto Main Street when a late model luxury sedan cut her off.

"Watch where you're going!" It was Lynette. "I have to get this document filed before five!" she said waving a stack of papers.

Agatha had been so excited to find the photo in the Baileys' living room, she forgot Mr. Bailey was working on a motion for the Dettmer case. That was probably the document Lynette was going to file!

With the mystery couple and their car now out of sight, Agatha gave up the chase.

As she pulled up to QGARST, Agatha heard the town bell chime five and wondered if Lynette had made it to the courthouse in time.

*   *   *

"I got the donation!" Agatha said as she entered QGARST.

"Thank you!" Andrea said. "M. Poirot enjoyed seeing Sam and was much better company than Mrs. Bailey could ever be. Why he even helped me organize the dog toys."

"He did?" Agatha said.

"He did. He put all of his favorites in one pile."

Agatha saw the terrier next to a mountain of dog toys he was pushing around with his snout. "It looks like all of them are his favorites."

"With the way Mrs. Bailey went on about how this had to be picked up today, I'm curious to see what's in it." Like a magician pulling rabbits out of a hat Andrea drew out one doily after another. "You're the expert, Agatha. Do any of these look interesting?"

"This one!" Agatha grabbed a doily with serpentine rows of stitches that meandered around other elements, "It's called Bruges crochet. It's a technique inspired by Bruges lace, and this doily looks just like one Eleanor gave me. Maybe it's another clue!" she said laughing.

"Another clue? Last I heard you were all out of clues."

"I was," Agatha said, "but while I was at the Baileys sleuthing—I mean waiting—Mr. Bailey said he was writing a motion connected to the Amelia Dettmer case."

"I would have thought he'd keep that under his hat, so to speak. How did you find out?"

"He thought 'the agency' had sent me as a replacement for a young woman who was quitting just as I got there."

Agatha then shared all of the goings on at the Bailey household including how Mr. Bailey had offered her $10 to watch Peaches.

"I wonder what's in that motion," Andrea said when Agatha finished her story.

"I do too. Speaking of the courthouse, could you watch M. Poirot tomorrow? I need to go to the clerk's office and look through the probate records."

"I'd love to," Andrea said, "but there's a board meeting late tomorrow afternoon. Mrs. Bailey and Lynette are looking to oust me so they can install someone of their choosing. Neither of them is on the board, but they have the ear of the president, and I need to be ready for whatever nonsense they throw my way. I'm going to have to spend all tomorrow morning preparing.

*   *   *

The next morning Agatha hurried to the kitchen to ask Mildred if she could watch M. Poirot, but when she got downstairs there was no Mildred, just a note on the kitchen table written in her familiar handwriting:

"I'll be out of town for two days as my sister broke her arm and needs surgery. Don't forget to feed M. Poirot."

As if he would let her, Agatha thought.

Discouraged, Agatha made a pot of coffee and put a piece of bread in the toaster. She tried not to ruminate on what she didn't have—a dog sitter for M. Poirot—and instead put her energy and effort on what she did have—a phone book. This, she thought as she turned the delicate pages, belonged in the Historical Society Museum.

As she carefully paged through the book she found the phone numbers of Mildred's home repair network recorded in a "notes" section in the front. The handwritten comments included the names of spouses and children along with important dates in their lives. It was a handwritten database that allowed Mildred to launch a charm offensive whenever the historic register home needed attention.

So this, Agatha thought, is how Mildred is always first in line with the repair people.

Intrigued by the notes on both the official "notes" page as well as those in the margins, Agatha forced herself to stay focused on the mission at hand, and turned to the "D's." In short order, she had run through every Dettmer in the Quercus Grove phone book.

All two of them.

Undeterred, she expanded her search to other villages and towns in Madison County and came up with three more, but it seemed Lydia might be right—maybe Amelia Dettmer's only relations resided in the many cemeteries that dotted Madison County.

"Is it possible," Agatha wondered aloud, "that no one on the planet is related to Amelia Dettmer?"

While Agatha pondered whether or not it was possible for a single human being to not be related to any one of the other eight billion people on the planet, M. Poirot finished eating his breakfast and barked, interrupting Agatha's thoughts.

"So do you want an adventure?" Agatha said to the terrier. "Well I've got an adventure for you!" After a quick walk around the block, she grabbed the bowling ball bag, put M. Poirot in the basket on her bicycle, and the two of them headed to the Historical Museum & Society.

After a short ride they reached their destination.

Agatha opened the bag. "You need to get in here."

M. Poirot snarled, then caught a whiff of the treat she had stowed in the bottom. He climbed in nose first.

Agatha locked her bike, then cautiously approached the entrance, crossed her fingers, and opened the door.

For the second time in as many days, Agatha found herself face-to-face with Mrs. Bailey.

"Hello, Agatha!" M. Poirot wriggled. "That's an interesting purse. It looks like a bowling ball bag."

"So it does!" Agatha said.

"How can I help you?"

Mrs. Bailey was one of the last people Agatha wanted helping her, but she had no choice. "I came to look at land records," she said. What she didn't say was that the land records in question were cemetery plots.

"Land records are over there." Mrs. Bailey pointed to the map room. "If you need help, just ask."

What Agatha really needed was for someone who wasn't named Bailey to be the volunteer on duty so she could look at the cemetery records. She lingered in the main room looking at the display of books for sale on the off chance that Mrs. Bailey would be called away, and she could sneak a look at the cemetery records she had come to see.

She read the title of each book twice and the blurbs on the back of at least half of them, but then M. Poirot squirmed, and she felt she had dawdled as long as she dared. She gave up any hope of looking over the cemetery records and made her way to the map room.

Agatha chose a drawer that was both out of Mrs. Bailey's line of sight and wouldn't require her to bend over with her dog-filled bag. She found herself looking at a map with parcels of land that had the same names affixed to them as many of the headstones she'd seen at St. James Cemetery.

From the maps she learned the Bigelows and Dettmers had been close neighbors as had the Baileys. She even found some Frickensteins and a very long list of names that were unfamiliar to her.

Remembering Abigail said Mrs. Bailey was not a Pioneer of Quercus Grove, Agatha searched the various land parcel maps for anyone with the last name of Kelly. She was unable to find anything. While it didn't confirm that Mrs. Bailey was not a Pioneer of Quercus Grove, it suggested that at least one side of her family was not.

Having looked at as many maps as was comfortable while toting M. Poirot in the bowling ball bag, Agatha found a chair where she could sit with the bag on her lap. Sitting down gave the dog more freedom of movement and allowed Agatha to continue her search while keeping an ear out for anything Mrs. Bailey might say. She began going through the land parcel books that were within arm's reach starting on the left and moving toward the right.

Agatha learned a lot from the land parcel books. Many of the names she came across were familiar, and she discovered that many of her classmates were probably descendants of a number of Madison County pioneers, but there were just as many names that had been lost to history.

Here and there she would find an item that piqued her interest, but with M. Poirot in her bag, she couldn't reach into it for a notebook or her phone. Instead she stretched her middle-aged brain and tried to memorize the information she thought might be important.

M. Poirot who had settled in nicely after finding another snack began to stir when Mrs. Bailey came into the map room to check on Agatha. Apparently he had also learned to identify her footfall.

"Are you sure I can't help you?" Mrs. Bailey asked as she looked to see what maps and land records Agatha was examining.

"Yes," Agatha said, "in fact…." As she was about to tell a prodigious lie they were interrupted by the tinkle of the bell over the door followed by the click of high heels.

"Is there anyone here who can help me?" a voice demanded. "I need help right now!"

"Some people," Mrs. Bailey said, annoyed at both the intrusion and the visitor's lack of decorum. She returned to the main room before she could see what Agatha was researching.

As quickly as her situation with a contraband dog allowed, Agatha put away the land parcel books and made her way to the main room.

When she got there, she saw the loud nasal twang belonged to the woman from the cemetery.

"I need to get my hands on maps of the cemeteries here. Pronto!" the woman said to Mrs. Bailey, her words punctuated with the pop of her gum.

"Are you looking for a specific cemetery?" Mrs. Bailey asked, her eyes still on Agatha.

"As a matter of fact, I am," the woman said. "It's the one out past the frozen banana place."

"Madison County is home to more than seventy cemeteries," Mrs. Bailey said haughtily, "and more than one of them is north of the Dairy Maid. It could be Liberty Prairie, Belk, or Zimmerman. 'Out past the frozen banana place' doesn't narrow it down."

"Well, La-di-dah," said the woman. "It's the one with a gazebo. You know, where that old bird Dettmer was buried."

"Old bird, indeed!" Mrs. Bailey said in horror. Agatha stifled a laugh. No doubt she and Mr. Bailey had said much worse about the now dearly departed Amelia Dettmer.

"I will have you know," Mrs. Bailey said, pulling herself up to be as tall and imposing as she could muster, "Amelia Dettmer was my neighbor for over forty years!"

Now was a good time for Agatha to make her escape. "Thanks for everything!" Agatha said in a falsely cheery voice as she waved good-bye to Mrs. Bailey and made her way to the door. Then, when she was just a couple of feet from freedom, M. Poirot snarled.

"Did your bag just growl?" Mrs. Bailey asked, a puzzled look replacing her indignation.

"I don't think so," Agatha said. "It was probably my stomach."

To Agatha's relief, the visitor interrupted again.

"Hey, I was talking to you, and I need a map of that cemetery, right now!"

Mrs. Bailey put on a pretense of being attentive, but she continued to find excuses to look Agatha's way, and when she could not stare at her directly, she gave her a side-eyed look.

When Agatha and M. Poirot finally got out of the Historical Society, a wave of relief washed over her just like when she was working for The Agency and successfully dodged an actual bullet.

And, just like working for The Agency, there was no time to bask in the glory of her escape. She needed to get onto the next thing.

And the next thing, according to M. Poirot, was lunch and a proper walk.

After a quick ride home, Agatha fixed him a bowl of dog kibble that left him unimpressed.

He sat by his dish and stared into it, while Agatha fixed herself a peanut butter and jelly sandwich.

When she finally sat down to eat, M. Poirot came over and sat at her feet. "Arf," he said as he looked up at her in an effort to determine if she had something he would like better.

"I'm sorry," Agatha said, "all I have is this sandwich." She held it out to show him.

M. Poirot continued to sit at her feet as if he had been superglued to the floor.

"I'm pretty sure you won't like peanut butter," she said. He was unmoved.

"It will stick to the roof of your mouth," she assured him. He was as unimpressed with this new excuse as he had been with the previous one.

"Okay, you can try a bite," she said, tearing off a piece from the center, "but you probably won't like it." She placed it in his bowl.

After a brief hesitation, he left her feet and conducted a thorough inspection of the bit of peanut butter and jelly sandwich she had served. He smelled it first, then gingerly licked the morsel.

Deciding it was safe he took one careful bite then devoured it, completely ignoring the dog food. "Arf," he barked again.

"Eat your kibbles," Agatha told him, and for once, M. Poirot complied.

Sitting at the kitchen table Agatha surfed the Internet while she finished her sandwich. She was searching to find living people whose names matched those she had identified as being high-value research targets.

But M. Poirot was having none of it. As far as he was concerned, it was time for another walk.

"You win, M. Poirot," she said as she got his leash and the two of them headed out the door.

CHAPTER THIRTEEN

An Adventure

AFTER M. POIROT'S WALK, Agatha spent the afternoon reviewing her notes from their trip to the Historical Society Museum. There were dates she didn't recall exactly, names she had spelled incorrectly, and poorly reconstructed maps she had drawn by hand. Before she knew it the sun had set, and the day was done.

After a quick dinner for both herself and M. Poirot and an even quicker walk, she locked up the house and climbed the two flights of stairs to her room. The wi-fi reception in the attic was awful, so rather than try to surf the web to find inspiration, Agatha returned to the shelf filled with her collection of Nancy Drew books. Just as Lydia found a heroine in Agatha Christie, Agatha found one in Nancy. She read over the titles: *The Clue in the Diary, The Sign of the Twisted Candle, The Password to Larkspur Lane, The Message in the Hollow Oak.*

Agatha could certainly use a clue or a sign or a password or a message—anything to jump-start her investigation. All she had to go on were small snatches of overheard conversations between Lynette and her mother, some haphazard notes she had made after a visit to the Historical Society Museum, a hat made by the mysterious Sevilla which purportedly contained a coded message, a couple in a burgundy car lurking at every turn she made, and a missing headstone.

That was her case. Agatha went over the facts and one thing became glaringly clear. If she were going to solve the mystery of Amelia Dettmer's will, she needed to get to the Madison County Courthouse to find out what the peculiar term in William Dettmer's will had been.

*   *   *

The next morning Agatha awoke with a renewed sense of purpose. She made a pot of coffee, then—following Mildred's detailed instructions—assembled M. Poirot's breakfast. The smell must have reached him in his sleep, because when it was ready to serve, he sauntered into the kitchen with his nose in the air.

With breakfast done, she got to the first order of business—writing a list—but first, she needed to find her notebook.

She checked the bowling ball bag. She checked her favorite crochet bag. Finally she emptied the bag she took when she visited Abigail Rowen and found both the notebook and Abigail's copy of *Millinery* by Jane Loewen.

Agatha scribbled a short list into the notebook then settled down to read the treatise on hat making that she had inadvertently brought home.

"… one learns more from applying principles rather than mere perusal of them," Ms. Loewen asserted.

Inspired, Agatha got out her hooks and yarn, and tried a variety of crochet stitches she thought might work. None of them did, and before she knew it, it was late afternoon.

She was startled when the phone rang. It was Claudia returning her call from the previous day. Agatha explained her predicament and the paralegal agreed to watch M. Poirot while Agatha went to the clerk's office.

*   *   *

The next morning Agatha packed her things in a sleek, granny square bag that would easily fit into one of the coin-operated courthouse lockers. Then she unearthed a reusable grocery bag for M. Poirot's gear—including his 2-in-1 travel water bottle—and she and the terrier headed over to the Law Office of Marcus Hill.

"You might need this," Claudia said, handing Agatha a credit card.

"For what?" Agatha asked.

"In case you find what you're looking for and want to print out copies. I have a good feeling about this," she said winking.

Agatha checked her phone. The courthouse wouldn't open for twenty minutes. That was plenty of time to fortify herself with a cappuccino before she spent the morning looking at probate records.

When she arrived at The Coffee Shop the line spilled onto the sidewalk in front. Word had gotten out at the Chocolate & Coffee Festival that Sam was the best barista east of the Mississippi.

"You're in my way," a familiar voice rose above the noise. Agatha turned to see Lynette shouldering her way past a line of people ahead of her. She did not let the festive air deter her from her usual antics.

"Stop trying to cut," a man's voice rang out.

"Who even says that any more?" Lynette replied. "This isn't grade school."

"You're the one trying to cut," the unidentified person retorted. "You must think you're the teacher's pet."

"I assure you, I was never any teacher's pet," Lynette replied.

Agatha tried to stifle a laugh, but it came out like a choking sound. Before she knew it, the person Lynette had tried to cut in front of sprang into action. He positioned himself behind Agatha and firmly thumped her back with the heel of his hand. After knocking the wind out of her, he reached his arms around her waist and placed his fist right below her belly button.

If she were going to speak up, that would have been the moment, but before she could say anything, her would-be rescuer had grasped his fist tightly with his other hand and made a quick upward and inward thrust expelling the last bit of air she had in her lungs.

"You look really pale," he said.

No doubt, she thought. The line cutting avenger had nearly squeezed the life out of her. "I'm okay," she managed to say.

"Are you sure?" he asked.

"I'm sure," she said. "I just need a cup of coffee."

"Sit down. I'll get it for you," Dudley Do-right said, as he pulled a chair out for her at an available table. "What do you want?"

"A cappuccino." Agatha took cash out of a crochet change purse she had picked up in Turkey and handed it to him. "Leave the change as a tip," she said. "Please."

While Agatha sat at a table, Lynette, relegated to the back of the line, fumed. The longer she stood, the faster she tapped her foot.

Meanwhile, Agatha's would-be rescuer was ushered to the front of the line by people happy to see Lynette get a long overdue comeuppance.

In no time, Agatha had her coffee.

"Thank you," she paused hoping he would fill in with his name. If he got her hint at all, he ignored it.

"My name is Agatha. Agatha Bigelow. And you are?"

"Adam," he said.

"Well, Adam," she said, "Thank you for your help. Especially the cappuccino."

His mood shifted. "Can we talk privately?"

Suddenly Agatha realized the meeting she was having was not an accident. Adam was trying to make contact. Her face flushed. She had only been separated from The Agency for a couple of months, and she had already lost her edge.

"How private is privately?" She was curious what he had to say for himself, but not curious enough to put herself in any greater peril than she might already be in.

"A public place where we can talk without being overheard. A place where Lynette isn't," Adam said.

"Do you know where Weldon's Bicycle Shop is?" Agatha asked,

"I saw it on my way into town."

"You leave first, and I'll meet you there. Ask Stan about bicycle rentals while you wait for me."

In a moment, Adam was out the door. Agatha would be surprised if she saw him when she got to the bike shop, but maybe he was on the up and up. Or maybe he was here to end her life because ending her career wasn't enough. Either way she was going to enjoy the cappuccino in case it was her last.

A few minutes later, Agatha slipped out the back of The Coffee Shop to an alley. The coast seemed clear, but she knew things aren't always what they seem.

"Hi, Stan," Agatha greeted the shop owner when she walked through the door. Adam was already there, and he and Stan seemed to be deep in conversation.

"Hi, Agatha, I'll be with you in a minute."

She sidled over to the counter where they were talking and listened for anything that might give her a clue who Adam (if that was even his name) really was.

"So if I rent the bike, can I rent a helmet too, or do I have to buy one?" Adam sounded so interested Agatha almost believed him.

"You can rent one," Stan said, "but I have to warn you, our rentals are distinctive." He pointed to a wall of helmets decorated in psychedelic colors.

"Do you have anything that doesn't stand out as much?" Adam asked.

"We have a collection of more neutral designs for sale over there."

"You look like you know your stuff." Adam said, smiling at Agatha, "Is there one you would recommend?"

"Let's look!" she replied.

Agatha was impressed with Adam's ability to redirect the conversation and maneuver her to a more private place where they could talk without arousing any suspicion from Stan. Under the circumstances she didn't know if that was good or bad.

"What kind of biking do you plan to do?" she asked.

"I want to be able to bike around the county and see what there is to see."

"Pleasure, or work?" she asked

"Work," he said ruefully. "Sandy beaches are more my idea of pleasure."

"Do you have a favorite sandy beach?" Agatha asked trying to learn more about him.

"No. I like every sandy beach."

"So what kind of work are you doing?"

"Investigating agricultural espionage."

Agatha's eyes widened—espionage? In Madison County? "Sounds interesting." She walked over to the wall of helmets and selected one in an aggressively neutral slate gray. "I think you'll find this offers you the protection you want but won't interfere with your peripheral vision so you can keep any would-be agricultural spies in your line of sight."

"No would-be, I'm afraid. This is a documented ring of thieves. What we don't know is who they are working for. There's just one problem."

CHAPTER FOURTEEN

An Exciting Discovery

"JUST ONE?" AGATHA said.

"Just one." Adam hesitated. "A few years ago I was on vacation." He paused again. "I went to a marketing presentation for what turned out to be a timeshare scam."

"And?"

"And I recovered most of my investment," he said, "but I had to testify in the criminal case. One of the people involved in the agricultural espionage is the woman I testified against. She said if she ever saw me again, she'd make sure I regretted it. When I realized she was one of the crooks I'm supposed to tail, I talked to an old friend from law school and that's when your name came up."

Agatha didn't need one more thing to do, but she couldn't pass up the opportunity to get back in the espionage game.

She'd show them. "This woman," Agatha said, "does she have big blonde hair and a strong nasal accent?"

"How did you know?" he said, surprised.

"The past few days, I've seen her all over Quercus Grove. In fact, the first time I saw her was at St. James Cemetery. She's got a sidekick—some guy who walks with his hands in his pockets looking like he's whistling past a graveyard even when he's not near one. What exactly is the espionage they're involved in?"

"They're rose thieves," Adam said, "and they have inside information on a rose being developed right here in Quercus Grove.

There's a graveside service this morning at St. James Cemetery, and I expect them to be there this afternoon to get their hands on whatever flowers are left at the grave. Could you do reconnaissance and be my eyes and ears?"

"Okay," Agatha agreed. "How do I reach you?"

"Don't worry, I'll find you," Adam said with a smile.

Adam's answer did little to put Agatha at ease, but with one more thing on her plate, she didn't have time to worry.

"Hey, Stan, my tires are kind of low. Can I have one of these?" Agatha asked grabbing a tire pressure gauge from a basket. The words "Weldon's Bicycle Shop, Quercus Grove," were printed on the side.

"Sure," Stan said.

"Thanks!" she said as she bolted out the door. Once she had safely exited the bike shop she thought about her situation. Either there were rose thieves on the loose in Madison County, or a counter spy had gotten to her. Either way, she had work to do.

Agatha walked to the courthouse and breezed right through security. She was both overwhelmed and exhilarated at the thought of espionage going on in Madison County, why if she had known....

"Miss!" Her thoughts were interrupted by the security guard. "You can't take your bag downstairs." He pointed to a bank of lockers. "Just put a quarter in, turn the key, and take it with you."

"Where can I get change for the lockers?" she asked.

He pointed to an exit. "Head out that door, make a right, and go down one block. The bank will make change if you have an account there."

And if you don't have an account there? she wondered. Agatha looked at the clock. She needed a quarter now, not ten minutes from now.

She went to the information booth.

"Do you know where I can get a quarter?" she asked an earnest looking young man whose name tag read *Kenneth*.

He repeated the instructions the guard had given her.

She dug into her bag and found a dollar. "If you have a quarter, we could trade," she said holding out a one-dollar bill.

"That wouldn't be right." Kenneth said. "That'd be stealing on the job. I could get fired." His face fell at the thought of his imaginary future firing. Then his face brightened.

"Did you crochet your bag?"

"I did," she said.

"My grandma used to crochet. I would sit next to her while her shows were on, and her hands would fly. Could you teach me how?"

"Sure," Agatha said. "Here's my card." This day wasn't turning out any better than the day before.

The information clerk read her card. "Since you're going to teach me to crochet, we're kind of friends. New friends, but friends. And since we're friends it shouldn't be a problem if I let you use a quarter while you're in the courthouse." He laid a quarter on the counter.

"Thank you," Agatha said with relief. "I'll have this back to you before lunch!"

Finally Agatha made it through security, stuffed everything but her wallet into the locker, then went down the stairs to the County Clerk's office.

"Can I help you?" a voice behind a high counter greeted her.

"I'm looking for probate records."

"Over there!" A bright red fingernail pointed past two microfilm readers toward a bookcase filled with dark blue binders. "Look up the call number, write it down, and bring it to me. I'll get the microfilm."

"Thanks." Agatha followed the clerk's instructions to the letter, and soon she had the first film threaded through the reader. "How do I make copies?" Agatha asked.

"See that button?"

She didn't.

"Right there," from across the room, the clerk pointed to a green square on the lower right of the machine. "You push that button, and it will copy whatever is inside the lines." She used her magic laser red fingernail to outline the parameters.

Agatha printed a dozen pages, but there were dozens more to go, and she had to pick up M. Poirot before noon.

There was no way she could get it all done.

"Can I use your phone to make a local call?" Agatha said.

The clerk's eyes narrowed. "How local is local?"

"Marcus Hill's office."

"I shouldn't let you, but I suppose this once won't be a problem."

Agatha dialed Marcus's office. "Hi Claudia," she whispered, "I found the documents, but I need 45 minutes to print them out. Could you meet me at the courthouse?"

"Noon on the front steps? Got it!"

Agatha looked back at the clerk. She had another favor to ask. "Since I'm the only one here, could I use both microfilm readers?

"We don't have a policy on that," the clerk said, "but I can't see why it would be a problem."

Agatha set the second reader up with another roll of microfilm. Soon she got into a rhythm, whirr then print, whirr then print as she went between one machine and the other.

She resisted the urge to read through the probate records, but as the information on the microfilm whirred forward, she occasionally peeked as the words flew by. There were names, familiar and unknown, and as the images and text flew past, her mind took the fragments and attempted to construct a narrative.

All the information going past her eyes was just waiting to be synthesized and turned into an Agency report.

Old habits die hard, Agatha thought.

For thirty glorious minutes it was just Agatha, the clerk, and the whirr of the microfilm machines. Then Agatha pressed print on the last page of William Dettmer's will, carefully put the microfilm rolls back in their boxes, and placed them in a bin to be refiled.

She looked at the clock. She needed to hurry if she were going to meet Claudia on time.

"How do I pay for the copies?" she asked.

The clerk nodded toward a sign on the wall. "We don't take cash or checks, but we do accept debit and credit cards. There's a $2.50 transaction fee for the card. Then the first 50 pages you print out are fifty cents. Anything over 50 pages is 25 cents."

Then she gave the clerk the credit card Claudia had given her.

"I'll need to see some identification," the clerk said.

Agatha pulled out her license.

"Agatha Christine Bigelow. Is that your real name?" the clerk asked.

"Yes," Agatha said. "My mother is a huge fan of the mystery writer."

"Say, is your mom the lady who does those tours?"

"She is!" Agatha said in a falsely bright voice she hoped didn't sound false.

"I read about those trips of hers in *The Acorn* all the time. It seems like it would be so much fun. Have you been on one?"

"No, I haven't" Agatha said.

"You should go," the clerk advised. "If I didn't have to stay in Quercus Grove to take care of my mom's cats, I would have gone on that Orient Express one that just left."

"It's a pretty popular tour," Agatha said, looking at the clock.

"Here are your copies," the clerk handed her a pile of papers and her license just as someone walked through the door.

Agatha turned to look. It was Lynette's mother.

"Fancy meeting you here," said Mrs. Bailey.

"The total is $69.25" the clerk said.

"Those must be important documents if you're spending that kind of money on them," Mrs. Bailey said trying to sneak a look at the pages the clerk handed to Agatha.

"What can I help you with?" the clerk asked Mrs. Bailey.

"I'll have whatever she's having," she said.

"Now you know that's confidential. I can't tell you what she printed out any more than I can tell her what you've printed out." The clerk continued, "The records might be public, but not who's reading them. Kind of like the library. But different."

The clerk turned to Agatha, "I'll need you to sign this," she said pointing to the receipt. Agatha signed her name and tried to pretend that she wasn't interested in anything Mrs. Bailey might want to print out. Then the clerk returned the credit card.

"Thanks for all your help," Agatha said, her fingers crossed hoping the clerk would not mention Marcus Hill.

Then she turned to Mrs. Bailey, "I hope you find what you're looking for!" she said.

Not, she thought as she hurried out the door.

CHAPTER FIFTEEN

A Desperate Situation

WITH ONLY TWO minutes to get to the courthouse steps where she was supposed to meet Claudia, Agatha ran up the stairs and opened the locker. She pulled out her bag and squeezed all 217 pages of the freshly printed documents into it. A few of them got wrinkled, but she wasn't late.

Yet.

Agatha was almost past security when she remembered Kenneth's quarter. She made a mad dash back to the bank of lockers, grabbed the wayward coin, and scrambled to the information booth.

When she arrived, Kenneth was talking to a woman in a black suit. "Sorry to interrupt" Agatha said, sliding the quarter onto the counter. "Call me when you're ready for a lesson!"

She arrived at the top the courthouse steps panting as the clock chimed twelve. Claudia slipped the bag filled with

M. Poirot's things onto Agatha's free shoulder then deftly transferred the crabby terrier into Agatha's waiting arms.

He greeted her with a quiet snarl.

"Here's the credit card," Agatha said.

Looking first one way and then the other, Claudia asked "Did you get what you need?"

"I think so," Agatha whispered. "I still have to read the documents, but I need to get to the cemetery. Now."

"Who died?"

"No one I know," Agatha said, "but it seems there's an agricultural espionage ring right here in Madison County. M. Poirot and I are scheduled to work a surveillance mission at St. James Cemetery this afternoon."

"Really?" Claudia's eyebrows shot up and doubt crossed her face. "Where did you hear about this?"

"It's a long story," Agatha told her, "but we need to go before there's trouble."

"What trouble?"

Agatha didn't have time to answer before the click of Mrs. Bailey's heels on the marble could be heard.

"Oh," Claudia said.

Mrs. Bailey descended the stairs and headed straight for them. "Agatha," Mrs. Bailey said looking right through Claudia, "I need to talk to you."

Mrs. Bailey tried to sound friendly, but no one—not Agatha, not Claudia, and least of all M. Poirot—believed her.

"Sorry, Mrs. Bailey, but M. Poirot needs lunch."

"I really need to talk to you. Now." she said too emphatically for M. Poirot's taste.

He growled.

"Really, Mrs. Bailey," Claudia interrupted, "what could be so important M. Poirot can't eat lunch first?"

M. Poirot barked in agreement.

"Gotta go," Agatha waved good-bye to Claudia and Mrs. Bailey, then she and M. Poirot were off.

M. Poirot had been so cooperative that, on their way to the cemetery, Agatha stopped at the Dairy Maid to get him lunch.

"You don't want anything on the burger?" The young man taking the order looked horrified.

"That's how he likes them," she said, pointing to M. Poirot.

"One plain Jane coming up!"

After a short wait, they were on the road again.

Agatha pedaled into a headwind as they turned north. She had been active when she was with The Agency, but her new job as a dog sitter meant she got a lot more exercise. In addition to all of the bicycling, there were the times she had to chase M. Poirot when either his headstrong nature, a mental lapse on her part, or a combination of the two occurred. It was embarrassing to be outrun by a twelve-pound dog, but Agatha noted to herself that her times were improving.

When they reached the cemetery, she parked her bike next to the gazebo so they could sit in the shade it provided. Agatha took M. Poirot's burger from the bag and discovered—to their mutual horror—it was not the "plain Jane" burger of his dreams, but had extra onion. M. Poirot turned up his nose in disgust and barked in protest.

At least Agatha had remembered to pack his combination 2-in-1 travel bottle and she was able to fix M. Poirot a drink, which he lapped right up. He might starve to death, but he wouldn't die of thirst. Then they sat in the shade of the gazebo and waited.

Agatha distracted herself from the heat and M. Poirot's wrath by examining their surroundings—namely the gazebo. She noticed there were large patches of grayed wood where the paint had peeled off, and the entire structure was in need of a thorough sanding and several coats of paint.

Then her eyes landed on a notice with details of an upcoming meeting. Maybe she could get involved and help restore the gazebo to its original grandeur. Maybe … her reverie about future meetings was interrupted by the sound of tires on gravel.

She hoped it wasn't Michael Chavez. No doubt her reappearance at the cemetery would move her from the top of his "prime suspect in a grave desecration" list to the top of his "definitely guilty of stealing the Dettmer headstone" list.

She looked up.

It was *the* burgundy car!

As the car drove past the gazebo, Agatha was able to confirm it was the same couple she had seen all over Quercus Grove. They were everywhere Agatha was: the cemetery, the Baileys, Quercus Grove Assisted Living, the Historical Society Museum—she even saw them leaving the hardware store. Could Adam be right? Were they really agricultural spies sent by an evil mastermind to steal cut roses from graves?

Agatha was sure the sun must be getting to her.

She reminded herself there were people who toured graveyards as a hobby, and St. James had a reputation for being haunted. But people looking for a good scare or evidence of the supernatural came when it was closer to dusk. They didn't

show up in broad daylight in the middle of a Chocolate &
Coffee Festival.

Agatha scratched M. Poirot behind the ears and hoped it
looked like he and she were a normal dog and mistress.

The driver parked the car by a grave so new the awning was
still up. That, Agatha thought, must be the grave Adam was
talking about. She watched as the couple emerged from the car.
They walked around the grave of the recently departed — the
woman tenuously balanced on her high-heeled shoes while the
man paced with his hands in his pockets. After checking to see
if anyone was looking, the woman picked up a large bouquet
of flowers.

Could these be the agricultural spies Adam talked about?
Or, Agatha wondered, had she been set up?

She made mental notes of the scene unfolding in front of
her — the probable make of the car, the heights of the man
and the woman — and tried to determine if either one had any
distinguishing characteristics aside from the blonde's big hair.

Ensconced in her invisibility cloak of middle-age, the couple
didn't seem to notice Agatha or M. Poirot, and everything
would have been fine had M. Poirot not decided he needed to
take action.

The woman reached down to pick up another arrangement,
and, in an instant, the terrier pulled hard on his leash and broke
away. Agatha jumped from the gazebo and chased him. She
ran across graves of the Sanders and Kaysers and Hills, but
M. Poirot's forty foot head start put Agatha at a disadvantage.

He ran past the most famous grave in all of St. James Cemetery, that of Lottie Plum, esteemed Quercus Grove pioneer
who had been murdered in a field adjacent to the cemetery.

M. Poirot ran around a precarious headstone from the 1850s, then straight for the shade of the awning over the newly filled grave and the two rose thieves.

The appearance of the small dog startled the couple, and M. Poirot—not being quite done with his mischief—snatched the flowers the woman had culled from the display. Unable to wrest the bouquet from him the woman grabbed the handle of his leash and dragged the growling and determined dog into the car.

"Hurry up!" she yelled to the man. "We need to get out of here!"

In an instant, it was over.

Agatha's life flashed before her as she watched the couple drive away with M. Poirot.

Her mother would never forgive her, and when Agatha died from the shame of this misadventure *The Acorn* would lead with a story about how she had allowed her mother's dog to be dognapped from a haunted cemetery that anyone with sense would know not to loiter in.

As the car pulled away, Agatha used the only tool she had at her disposal—the camera on her phone—and she took a series of blurred photos as the dognappers sped toward town.

Knowing she needed to report the news of M. Poirot's dognapping immediately, she tried to call the police but the cellphone reception, which was usually spotty, was nonexistent.

Agatha ran back to the gazebo, climbed onto her bike, and began the long ride home.

In any spy novel, she thought, the thieves would have had trouble starting their car or gotten a flat tire, but this was real life, and no matter how hard Agatha pedaled, she got further and further behind. Soon, the increasingly smaller speck that was the getaway car grew smaller and smaller still until it disappeared completely.

Despite having the wind at her back Agatha's heart was heavy, her feet were like clay, and the road back to town looked miles longer than it was. How, she wondered, could she feel so miserable at the loss of a creature who loathed her with the might of a dog ten times his size? One thing was certain: there would be no way to explain to her mother that M. Poirot had been dognapped.

With her heart and her feet growing heavier with each push of the pedals of her bike, Agatha pressed forward toward town.

CHAPTER SIXTEEN

Left to Starve

M. Poirot did not go gentle into the good night that was his dognapping.

He barked, he yipped, he growled, and he made a noise unlike anything either the man or woman had ever heard.

"He's possessed!" the woman said.

"Then why did you take him?" the man asked. "Do you have any idea how much trouble we could get into?"

"I didn't 'take' him. I just didn't let the little thief run off with our roses!" she said.

"Now we'll need to feed him," the man said.

"Why?" the driver's companion snarled. "We can let him starve."

The driver looked at her in disbelief. "Do you have *any* idea what the penalties for animal cruelty are?"

"No." she said looking out the window.

"If we get caught and end up back in the clink, we will be toast."

"We are not going to get caught," the woman said, "because I'm NOT going back to prison. No hair color, no lipstick, and no manicures. No," she said, holding out her hand to admire her nails.

"You'd better hope not," her companion hissed, "you have no idea how hard prison life is if you hurt an animal. PETA has connections, and they will take you out."

She gave the driver a condescending sneer. "I don't know what 'pita' is, but you don't scare me any more than this rat masquerading as a dog," she said pointing to the terrier.

M. Poirot barked at her with renewed vigor. The woman grabbed a newspaper and swatted him with it which only made him bark more. He even added a snarl. She wasn't the only one who could condescend.

"Stop that!" her companion yelled.

"Don't you raise your voice to me!" she said.

M. Poirot and the driver went silent, uncertain which one of them she meant.

Finally the man spoke. "The way you're treating this dog, we're liable to get pulled over and arrested," he said. "We didn't come this far to have everything undone by a twelve-pound dog. Don't blow it."

"Oh, no!" she cried in horror.

"What, what's wrong?" The driver checked the rearview mirror. "Is the law after us?"

"No, it's worse than that!" the woman said. Tears streamed down her face, dissolving her ample mascara. "That dog," she said pointing at M. Poirot, "broke my nail!"

The three of them settled into a grim silence and stared at the road ahead.

As they neared town, the driver spoke.

"We need to find a place to unload this dog before he's the end of us then get something to eat and leave town."

"I don't need to eat," the woman hissed. "I need a nail salon. And not a cheap out of the way one. I need one with good technicians who can fix the damage this horrid creature did," she said, pouting. "One like that Cutting Edge place."

"So your idea of laying low is to go to a high-end salon in the middle of town with black mascara running down your face?" the man asked.

"Anyone with a brain will understand why I'm crying when they see this." She wagged the offending finger in his face. "And my mascara isn't black, it's navy blue."

The driver pulled into one of Quercus Grove's elusive two-hour parking spots and deftly parked the car. "I'll meet you back here in an hour," he said.

"It's a two-hour spot," she argued. "That's enough time to get my hair washed and my makeup redone," she said. "Then, if we do get caught, I'll look good for my mug shot."

"Are you crazy? We need to blow town, not move here."

"You know," she said with authority, "being in a hurry to get out of town makes you look guilty. That's the mistake I made when I was selling those beachfront time shares. If I'd've just stayed put, I never would've been caught!" She took a tissue from her purse and tried to wipe the mascara off her face. "If we take our time, then no one will suspect a thing."

The driver shook his head then grabbed the leash and got out of the car. "I'm going to get the dog re-homed. Be back in an hour."

"Whatevs, sweetheart," his companion said, blowing him a kiss.

M. Poirot, for one, was glad to be rid of the Cruella de Vil wannabe. He put his nose to the ground and soon smelled something familiar. He tugged on his leash to get the driver to come along. He followed his nose and led the man right to the front door of QGARST.

"I never even heard of a QGARST," the man said as he looked at the sign. But M. Poirot insisted and pulled on the leash even harder.

Andrea looked up when she heard the bell jingle. "M. Poirot, it's good to see you!"

The rose-thief-turned-dog-sitter grew uneasy. He was in a town of at least 20,000 people in the middle of a Chocolate & Coffee Festival that had brought in a couple of thousand more, and the first business he walked into, the clerk knew the dog by name.

This was not going as planned.

But his partner's erratic nature had taught him to think on his feet, so in just a couple of seconds he came up with what he hoped was a plausible lie. "I was wondering if you could help me out, here."

"I don't know," Andrea said. M. Poirot was now secure in her arms and had stopped growling.

"I was out at the cemetery down the road a ways, and darned if this little fella didn't run over to me when I was paying my respects to my father's granduncle."

Andrea made no motion. "Really?"

The rose thief tried to read her face, but she was not giving anything away.

"Yeah," he said, scratching his head in what he hoped was a good imitation of an innocent person, "I was there paying my respects to old Gottlieb, when this little fella came running over. I didn't see anyone with him, so I thought maybe I'd better bring him to town."

"He was alone?" Andrea asked.

"Yeah, I didn't see anyone with him." The man started sweating what he thought must be large, easily visible salty bullets. He hoped she wouldn't ask about how he just happened to have a leash. Then he felt his hands go cold and clammy.

He was getting too old for this stuff.

The woman who hired them promised it would be easy money and said there would be nothing to it. But this job had been anything but easy.

First, there was the Chocolate & Coffee Festival which made parking practically impossible. He already had a folder full of tickets. Then there was the matter of the dogs. They were all over the town, and not just this little rat looking one. It seemed that an old—really old—broad had up and died, and there was some kind of problem with the estate, and everybody was up in arms. And there were dogs as far as the eye could see.

Even the house they were surveilling had a dog. A huge dog. One that looked like a horse—a horse named Peaches. That, he thought for a moment, might be a good title for a movie.

Maybe when they finished with this job and got their money he could move to the outskirts of Palm Springs, get himself one of those trailers at a trailer park and a typewriter—or maybe some of those yellow note pads like his lawyers always used. He could write the story of his life, and if not his life, then he could write the story of a horse named Peaches, who wasn't really a horse, but was a very, very large dog.

Getting lost in his reverie about life after the rose heist calmed him down. His hands were no longer sweating, the river of his underarms had slowed to a trickle, but now he felt like he needed to explain his silence.

"Sorry," he said, the catch in his voice sounding almost genuine, "I was just thinking about my pops and his granduncle. Very moving."

"I can't thank you enough for bringing M. Poirot in. I know his owner will be very glad to get him back." Andrea forced a smile.

"To be honest, he more or less brought himself in." The rose thief shivered as he felt a chill come over him. It had been so long since he had told the truth, it felt weird. Not bad weird, but definitely not normal.

Andrea handed the man an index card. "Why don't you leave your name and address," she said, "I know his owner will want to thank you herself."

He paused for a moment, then recalled the name and address of an attorney who helped him stay out of jail a few years earlier, and he wrote it on the card she had given him so he would not look like some sort of criminal.

CHAPTER SEVENTEEN

Andrea Walker's Story

ANDREA WATCHED AS Gottlieb's alleged great grandnephew left QGARST. "Don't let the door hit you on the way out!" she thought.

She'd only been in town eight weeks, but eight weeks was long enough to know the guy was not a native of Quercus Grove and that anyone named Gottlieb buried in one of the local cemeteries scattered throughout the county was long dead and not a close relation to either him or his "pops."

Then, there was his ridiculous story about M. Poirot. The terrier was known for running away from people, not running to them. Did the guy really expect her to believe he was a doggy pied piper able to summon renegade terriers who would then obediently follow him? Still, she didn't challenge his story because she didn't know if he was armed and stupid or just stupid.

Andrea walked to the front window of the store and watched as he crossed the street, hands so deep in his pockets he looked like he was digging for gold. She didn't know what he was up to, but she was sure it was illegal, and she was determined to find out what it was.

She turned to M. Poirot who was trying to arrange a blanket to his satisfaction.

How had the man gotten his hands on the dog and what exactly had M. Poirot been through? When she first picked him up, his whole body trembled. But once he settled down, he gently licked her face in what she could have sworn was Morse Code. But even people didn't learn Morse Code these days. How would a dog know it?

Andrea knew her imagination was working overtime, but a town like Quercus Grove could do weird things to your mind.

She didn't think she would ever get used to the place.

*　　*　　*

It had been an otherwise ordinary day when a series of events was set in motion that upended Andrea's life.

"Walker, meet me in my office!" Moxley barked after a particularly contentious meeting. She did as he asked, but once he shut the door of his office, she felt certain he had just shut the door on her future.

"I've got an interesting assignment for you," he said. "Ever heard of," he looked at the sheet of paper on his desk, "Quercus Grove?"

Arms folded, she shook her head no.

"If you play your cards right, it could lead to a big promotion."

Andrea didn't like conditional metaphors. They almost always meant the exact opposite of what was being said. The truth was this: if she had the right cards to play, she would be going to Miami or San Francisco or Honolulu. Not Quercus Grove—population 20,753.

"You'll be a Director!" Moxley said, trying to sell her on the idea.

"Director of what?" she asked, her arms still crossed.

He peered over his glasses to read the paper he held in his hand, "Director of Q-G-A-R-S-T, a trendy mission-driven thrift store located in historic downtown Quercus Grove."

Andrea was not trendy, and while she wanted to dismiss him completely, the phrase "mission-driven," piqued her interest.

* * *

"Arf !" M. Poirot's bark interrupted Andrea's trip down memory lane.

Like the cemetery where this guy's alleged great granduncle was buried, Quercus Grove was the kind of place careers went to die.

"You're right," she said as she scratched the terrier behind his ear, "We need to find out what Gottlieb's great grand nephew is up to when he isn't 'rescuing' dogs."

Andrea continued to pet M. Poirot, and tried to recall anything uniquely identifiable about the man who brought the terrier in, but almost everything about him was nondescript. His hair (brown), his face (somewhere between oval and round), his eyes (gray or hazel), his glasses (did he even wear any?), his clothes (khaki pants, a plaid shirt, and scuffed leather shoes).

There was one thing that was distinctive: his accent—more eastern seaboard city slicker than Midwest farmer. She didn't know what had brought him to Quercus Grove, but whatever it was, she knew it wasn't anything good.

Andrea read over the information he provided on the index card to see if there was anything she could learn, but even his name—Chris Perry—was nondescript. He could be from anywhere. He had listed his home address as a Thompson Street in Hackensack, New Jersey. Something about the name and address seemed familiar, but she couldn't think of what it was. She would have to look into it later. Right now she needed to get to the police station with M. Poirot so she could file a report.

She wasn't certain a crime had been committed, but she wanted to get her story on the record.

One of the few upsides of the Quercus Grove assignment was that she was living in the same town as her old college chum, Roscoe Edwards, who just happened to be the new editor of *The Acorn Register.*

They had bumped into each other at the Coffee Shop her first week in town and swapped stories about where they had been and what they had done.

It was a far cry from the life she had imagined for them: she as the first woman Director of the FBI, and he as the editor of a national newspaper, inviting her to write guest op-ed pieces on matters of national security. They had been best friends, and over a cup of coffee where he peppered her with questions about her ambitions for both herself and QGARST, she realized how much she missed the inside jokes and camaraderie they shared when they were young.

Yes, Andrea thought, she needed to get this story on the record so if there was more to it, Roscoe could assign a reporter to look into it further.

Andrea sighed then placed the pen and index card into a plastic bag and put it in her purse. It wasn't the most forensically sound option, but she needed to work with what she had. A description of a guy who looked like almost every other guy in the Midwest, a dog as witness to whatever crimes the guy might have committed, and maybe, just maybe, one good fingerprint.

Andrea was looking for her keys when M. Poirot barked at the jingle of the bell over the door as it opened.

Not now, Satan, she thought.

When Moxley read the job description to her, there had been nothing about managing Lynette Bailey. Unfortunately, it was at least a quarter of the job, and with M. Poirot's unexpected arrival Andrea didn't have time for any of Lynette's antics or her new pet project—a customer's bill of rights. Inspired by the events surrounding Agatha's purchase of the vintage cloche, she was in almost daily to report on her progress.

Andrea looked up, ready to tell Lynette she didn't have time for her nonsense when, to her surprise, Agatha Bigelow walked through the door. She was panting and looked stricken.

"Andrea, you'll never believe what happened!"

"Try me," she said.

Before Agatha could say anything, M. Poirot bounded over to Agatha, stood at her feet, and barked.

"Look!" Andrea said, "he's glad to see you!"

"If by 'glad' you mean furious, then yes, he looks very glad to see me." Agatha picked him up. "Good to see you," she cooed. M. Poirot continued to bark and growl.

It seemed to Andrea he was trying to tell Agatha what had happened to him.

"I have to know, Andrea, where did you find him?"

"I didn't find M. Poirot—he found me," she said.

"How?" Agatha asked.

"He walked right through the door with a man I've never seen before."

"Not a man with a woman?"

"No, just an ordinary looking guy who says is name is Chris Perry," Andrea said. "He told me he had been out at a cemetery to pay his respects to his Great Granduncle Gottlieb, and M. Poirot just ran up to him."

"Well if it's the same guy who was out at St. James Cemetery, that's not how it happened," Agatha said.

"Do tell!" Andrea said, glad to have accurately identified the man as being up to no good.

"I'm doing research for Marcus Hill," Agatha began.

"Isn't he the attorney handling Amelia Dettmer's estate?" Andrea asked.

"Yes, he is," Agatha said.

According to Roscoe, it was rumored that a clause in the will that put the entire future of QGARST—including Andrea's position as director— at stake. She hoped Agatha would say more.

"As a matter of fact, my research is how M. Poirot got kidnapped."

"Go on," Andrea encouraged her.

"When I was looking at the probate documents Marcus shared with me, it was clear the 'peculiar' clause in Amelia's will is related to the terms of her father's will. So I went to the Clerk of Court this morning to see if there was anything in William Dettmer's probate records that would shed light on the whole 'living relation' business, and I think I hit pay dirt."

Agatha patted the crochet tote full of the documents she printed out. "After I finished at the Clerk of Court, I thought it would be a good idea to take another look at Amelia's grave. We were sitting in the shade of the gazebo when a burgundy car pulled in. The driver parked the car next to the awning of a new grave, and then he and the blonde he was with got out. Maybe you've seen her," Agatha said. "She has really big hair, and she wears high heels all the time."

"How do you know she wears high heels all the time?" Andrea said.

"I've seen the two of them all over town — at the assisted living facility, driving past the Baileys', and coming out of the hardware store. She always has heels on. I'm surprised she hasn't checked out the selection here."

Andrea's eyes narrowed. "Are you sure they aren't following you?"

"Why would anyone follow me?" Agatha said. "I'm just a middle-aged as-yet-undiscovered crochet designer living in a garret in the house my great grandfather built."

"So you don't think they were there to visit his mysterious 'Uncle Gottlieb'?"

"No," Agatha said firmly. "If someone named Gottlieb had died in Madison County, he would've been at least 123 years old, and his death would have knocked Amelia Dettmer's off the front page. Anyway, the woman looked like she was picking through the flowers. Whatever she was doing, M. Poirot didn't like it. He tugged on his leash and started running. He got ahead of me, and I never caught up." Agatha watched the terrier as he busily munched on the hamburger he had earlier refused to eat.

"M. Poirot went straight to the woman and tried to take what she had in her hand, and then they got into a fight. She grabbed his leash, and the next thing I knew, she was throwing M. Poirot into the back seat of the car and yelling to her partner that they needed to step on it. He got in on the driver's side, started up the car, and they pulled out of the cemetery and headed west. I tried to call the police, but I couldn't get any cell service, so I rode straight back to town."

"Now," Agatha said with a sigh, "I need to report the dognapping, and I decided to stop by and see you before I went to the police station…. With the way my day has gone, I'm sure Steven Hughes will be the officer on duty, and I don't feel like talking to him."

"Well," Andrea said, "You need to report this crime, and I'm going to come with you."

CHAPTER EIGHTEEN

Notifying the Police

A GATHA AND M. POIROT waited in front of QGARST while Andrea placed a sign in the window informing any customers that the thrift store would be closed for an hour. "We don't want anyone breaking in and absconding with the dog toys, now do we? Andrea said to M. Poirot as she checked the door to make sure it was locked tight.

"See you at the police station," she said as she waved good-bye to the duo.

With that, Agatha plopped M. Poirot into his basket, then double- and triple-checked his seat belt. It wouldn't look good if he got away from her on their way to the police station to report his dognapping. She knew if Steven Hughes were the officer on duty, he would find a reason to cite her.

With M. Poirot at the helm, Agatha and the terrier zigged and zagged past the open trenches of the new sewer system being installed. Despite the construction and a couple of detours, they reached the entrance of the Quercus Grove Police Department in record time. And, thanks to Agatha's advocacy, there was a new bike rack where they could park.

Agatha reviewed her story as she locked her bike. She needed to report the dognapping—she did not need to report the agricultural espionage.

Explaining to Steven that an operative known only to her as "Adam" asked her to investigate at the cemetery would only further cloud the issue. He would want to know how she knew the operative and what she was investigating. When she had what she considered the pertinent facts of the story in order, she grabbed M. Poirot and the two of them marched into the police station.

"You can't bring your dog in here!" Steven said pointing to the "only service dogs allowed" sign behind him.

As she had feared, Steven Hughes was the officer on duty.

"But he's the victim of a crime!" Agatha said.

"What happened? Did some body steal his bone?" Steven said sarcastically.

M. Poirot growled.

"Hey," Steven said, in his getting-back-to-business voice, "I could cite you for that."

"Being an animal does not mean you can't be the victim of a crime," Agatha said, "and if you must know, he was dognapped."

"There's no such thing as 'dognapping,'" Steven said.

"What do you mean?" Agatha said. "He was taken against his will!"

"If he was 'dognapped,' as you say, why is he with you?" Steven asked.

"The dognapper took him into QGARST and left him with the new director, Andrea Walker."

"That doesn't change the fact that dogs are not allowed in here if they aren't certified service animals. It also doesn't change the fact that the taking of a dog is not a violent crime—it is a property crime. Kidnapping involves depriving a "person" of their liberty. A dog is (a) not a person, and (b) cannot be "deprived" of liberty. In fact, Code 1978, (a) states: all dogs shall be kept under restraint. The whole point of that code is to deprive a dog of liberty. Besides, if I'm not mistaken, M. Poirot is your mother's dog."

"What does that have to do with it?" Agatha said.

"That means neither you nor the dog are a victim of a crime. M. Poirot is your mother's dog. She's the real victim here, and she'll have to file the report."

"She's traveling, so I have to report the crime," Agatha argued. "And I can't leave him in my bicycle basket because that would be abandonment!"

"He's still not allowed in the police station," Steven insisted.

"Then why don't you come outside to take the report," a new voice chimed in. It was Andrea.

"If I were you, miss, I wouldn't get involved in this."

"What did you just call me?" Andrea's eyes narrowed, and she crossed her arms.

"I didn't call you anything," Steven said.

"Yes you did. You called me 'miss.' I'll have you know, I'm a grown woman. I am not anyone's 'miss,' and I will *not* tolerate that kind of nonsense. A crime has been committed, and you are refusing to take a report. That is dereliction of duty and a violation of your oath. I'm sure my good friend Roscoe Edwards, editor of *The Acorn Register*, will be interested to hear that when two citizens of this town come to the police station to report a crime, the police officer on duty can refuse to take a report because the victim is a dog."

"Just so you know, it's against the law to have the dog in this building, but under the circumstances I guess I have no choice but to let you make your report here." Steven turned to Agatha. "But don't let him get away, or I will cite you."

Then he pulled out a notebook and pen and faced two angry women and an even angrier dog. "So, what happened?" he asked.

Agatha and Andrea exchanged glances, then Agatha began.

"I had work to do at the courthouse this morning, and because I didn't have anyone to watch M. Poirot, Marcus Hill's paralegal, Claudia, agreed to take him." Agatha looked to see if Steven believed her story. He was busy taking notes and didn't even look up. "When I picked him up, Claudia said he deserved a treat for being so good."

"Go on," he said.

"He loves riding in the basket on my bicycle, so I thought he would enjoy a ride out in the country after being inside all morning," she continued. "He was hungry so we stopped at the Dairy Maid, and I got him a hamburger."

"What kind?" Steven asked.

"What do you mean, what kind?" Agatha said.

"What kind of burger did you get him," Steven said. "You know, cheese, bacon…."

"Just a bun and meat," Agatha said. "The cashier called it a 'plain Jane.'"

"Plain Jane," Steven said to himself as he dutifully wrote down the information.

"When the order was ready, we continued out toward St. James Cemetery, and arrived around one o'clock. It was warm. I parked by the gazebo so we could sit in the shade, and I fixed M. Poirot a drink of water."

"Where did you get water?" Steven said.

"I brought it with me," Agatha said. "FYI, not giving an animal in your care water is neglect which is a Class-B felony punishable with up to six months in jail."

"What about his burger?" Steven asked.

"He wouldn't eat it because it had onions on it."

"You just told me you ordered him a 'plain Jane,'" Steven said, reading from his notes.

"They made a mistake on the order," Agatha said. She glared at Steven then continued, "I was just giving M. Poirot a good scratch behind his ears when a burgundy car pulled into the cemetery."

"Burgundy?" Steven interrupted.

"Burgundy," Agatha said matter-of-factly.

"You're sure it wasn't maroon?"

She pulled out her phone and showed him a photo of the car as it pulled out of the cemetery.

"I know that car!" Steven said with excitement. "I've written five tickets for it since the Chocolate & Coffee Festival started. You'd think they'd learn after the third or fourth ticket, but no. By the way, that car is definitely maroon, not burgundy."

Agatha was annoyed. Here M. Poirot had been dognapped, and Steven was splitting hairs about the color of the getaway vehicle.

And he was wrong.

"It's not the first time they've been out to St. James Cemetery," she said. "In fact they were there the day of that huge thunderstorm."

Steven scribbled furiously in the notebook.

"I thought it was odd they pulled up when they did, but I wasn't paying too much attention because M. Poirot and I were on the gazebo in the old part of the cemetery, and the car was over in the new part parked next to a grave that still has the awning up."

"That's Mr. Brown," Steven said.

"Was Mr. Brown's first name Gottlieb?" Andrea asked.

"No, his first name was Arnold. He was the youngest son of old John Henry Brown," Steven said. "Why would you think his name was Gottlieb?"

"Because that's what the dognapper told me!" Andrea said glaring at Steven.

"Technically, if he did take the dog, he's a dog thief, not a dognapper. Now what do you mean, that's what he told you? You saw the dognapper?—I mean thief."

"Yes," Andrea said. "The man who brought M. Poirot into QGARST told me he was out at the cemetery paying his respects to his father's Granduncle Gottlieb when out of nowhere, M. Poirot ran over to him."

"When did he come into QGARST?" Steven asked.

"A little over an hour ago," Andrea said, annoyed.

"Today?" Steven asked.

"Yes, today!" Andrea said. "He waltzed in with the dog like he didn't have a care in the world. Of course, I recognized M. Poirot immediately and said hello. Then I asked the man how he happened to have M. Poirot, and he claimed he found the dog out at the cemetery. He failed to tell me that by 'found' he meant dognapped. I might have even managed to get a fingerprint or two," Andrea said holding up the plastic bag with the index card.

"Where did you get this?" Steven said.

"I suggested there might be a sizable reward, and I asked the dognapper to write down his name and address in case M. Poirot's owner wanted to contact him."

"Wait," Steven said, "what reward?"

"There isn't really a reward," Andrea said. "I was just trying to get a good fingerprint and possibly a name."

"You mean you lied to him?!" Steven said, aghast.

Steven abandoned his notebook and pen and switched to his computer and opened a software program that allowed him to construct a timeline of events. "So, he came to QGARST a little over an hour ago."

He continued to pepper them with questions, and used the time stamps on the photo Agatha had taken and the parking tickets he had issued, to create a "crime line."

Then, using another feature of the software, he input the addresses of the locations where the couple or the car had been spotted—the cemetery, the Baileys, QGARST, QGHM&S, along with the coordinates where all of the tickets had been issued—and created what he called a "crime map."

"Since you don't believe us that they dognapped M. Poirot, how do you know they've committed a crime?" Andrea asked.

"They've been in town for less than a week, and they've already racked up five parking tickets. These are experienced criminals," Steven said.

Agatha thought experienced criminals would try to avoid getting parking tickets, but she also knew parking in downtown Quercus Grove was a nightmare. She was sure the Chocolate & Coffee Festival had not made it any easier.

Steven started to read back the statement so Agatha and Andrea could make corrections.

"Where is that?" Andrea asked, pointing to a spot on the crime map. "It looks like two of those tickets are in almost the same place."

"Near the intersection of Main and Second," Steven said.

Agatha looked at Andrea. "Let's go!" they said in unison.

Before Steven could finish reading the statement the trio was out the door.

"You need to read and sign this before I can file the report," Steven said as he stood in the doorway, "and I have to warn you," he said, "there is no such crime as dognapping in this state, so I can only arrest them for the parking tickets."

"We'll be back," Agatha assured Steven, but if these two scoundrels are still in town, we need to find them now!"

"I better get back to QGARST," Andrea said to Agatha. "I expect our dognapper and his friend might come to the store. You know, just in case he left something behind."

She held up a set of keys and winked.

CHAPTER NINETEEN

A Risky Undertaking

Agatha and Andrea conferred outside the police station and hastily devised a plan to catch the dognappers. Andrea would go back to QGARST to wait for the man to come looking for his keys, while Agatha and M. Poirot would search the streets of downtown Quercus Grove for the dastardly criminals who had abducted the terrier.

With M. Poirot's leash secured to his collar, Agatha looped the handle around her wrist. Now if he tried to make an escape, she would have a better chance to stop him.

The only thing left was to change her appearance.

She rummaged through her purse and found the oversized sunglasses her ophthalmologist advised her to wear to slow the progression of cataracts. They were in a case under the tire pressure gauge she had picked up from Weldon's bike shop. She had hoped to put air in her tires, but with the addition of agricultural spies to investigate and M. Poirot's subsequent dognapping she hadn't had a chance to go to the gas station.

With her big sunglasses on and the little dog in tow, Agatha turned her head and walked with mincing steps in what she hoped was a convincing middle-aged Hollywood ingenue sort of way occasionally admonishing M. Poirot in a breathless voice.

She followed his lead as he meandered through the central city park where he was determined to leave no stone, twig, leaf, or scrap of paper unturned. It only took them twelve minutes to walk across the park, but every sniff of the ground and tug of the leash made it seem that it was taking much longer.

They were still a block and a half from QGARST when the terrier stopped dead in his tracks and growled.

"Oh, Sampson," Agatha said with a breathy affect. She knew from Andrea's account at least one of the dognappers knew M. Poirot's name, so she didn't dare use it. After giving her a withering doggy stare, M. Poirot—aka Sampson—went back to what had caught his attention in the first place: a late model, burgundy sedan parked a few feet ahead.

In one of Quercus Grove's elusive two-hour parking spots.

It sure looked like the car Agatha had seen out at the cemetery and driving past the Baileys.

But who, she wondered, would stick around town after committing a dognapping?

It made no sense.

Maybe the guy thought Andrea had believed his story and didn't realize he'd been busted.

Agatha had a plan, but before she could implement it, she needed to confirm she had the right car. She got out her phone, and took a photo of M. Poirot to create a cover for the two of them, then she checked the photo she took as the couple drove away from the cemetery. It looked like the right car, but she wasn't sure. Then she found a distinctive dent on the back bumper. It was there in the pictures, and the same dent was on the car right in front of her.

It wasn't just any burgundy four-door sedan; it was *the* burgundy four-door sedan. M. Poirot had found the car. She sent Andrea a text with the news along with coordinates of the car's location.

Then Agatha and M. Poirot proceeded to search the immediate vicinity while Agatha implemented her plan to stop the rose thieves from making another get away.

After surveilling the area as nonchalantly as she could, she went to the back tire on the passenger's side of the car, reached down, unscrewed the cap on the tire valve stem, and used her new tire gauge to "check" the air pressure. Soon she heard the satisfying hiss of air escaping.

She put the cap back on the valve stem, when she was sure there was enough air out of the tire that the warning light would come on when the driver tried to start the car. Then, to make certain they'd need to find a gas station with a working air pump before leaving Quercus Grove, Agatha did the same to the back tire on the driver's side.

With two of the tires deflated, Agatha pretended to look at her reflection as she peered into the car windows to see if she could find any evidence that might confirm what these crooks were up to. In the back seat—mixed in with candy bar wrappers, soda cans, a pair of pruning shears, gardening gloves, and a pair of binoculars—was a collection of roses in various stages of wilting.

There were pink roses and yellow roses and red roses and a rose that looked just like the ones that surrounded the Baileys' porch.

The assortment of roses explained why Agatha had seen the couple out at the cemetery and driving past the Baileys' house. It didn't explain what they were doing with the roses or who the mastermind behind the crime was, but it seemed that Adam really was in Madison County to investigate agricultural espionage and not on a mission to take her out.

While M. Poirot inspected the ground, Agatha looked at the nearby shops. When they neared the door of QGARST, M. Poirot's tail went up, and he began to sniff in earnest. Then he pulled Agatha across the street toward Quercus Grove's trendiest salon—Cutting Edge.

Cutting Edge was too fashion forward for Agatha. The last time she had gone to a salon this trendy it had taken her a year to grow out the layers. Still the salon did a booming business without her. With each sniff, M. Poirot tugged harder at his leash.

"This makes no sense," she whispered to M. Poirot. "Who would stop at a salon after committing a crime like dognapping?"

He looked up his nose at her with an air of disbelief.

Still not convinced he had found what they were looking for, Agatha strolled past the salon and peered into the shop window. She pretended to read the posted list of services and beauty products. Her eyebrows went up in surprise when she saw the cost of a shampoo and blow dry. It would be a long time before she could get her hair done here, but the menu of services did give her the opportunity to surveil the salon. She was startled to see the man from the cemetery sitting in the waiting area.

Common sense told her she was wrong, but her eyes said he was the guy. She snapped a photo of the suspect, and sent it to Andrea.

A bubble of dots immediately emerged. "That's the dognapper!" Andrea texted back. Then more bubbles. "Where did you find him?"

"At Cutting Edge."

Tired of standing around, M. Poirot tugged at his leash just as a woman emerged from a station in the back of the salon. It was the rose thief turned dognapper. Agatha kept a firm grip on his leash while she listened as the woman argued with the receptionist over the bill.

"You charged me for a whole manicure! That's not right. I only needed one nail done!" the woman yelled. The receptionist turned to the menu of services on the wall and pointed to the policy on nail repair.

"I only had to have them all redone because you didn't have the right color nail polish!" Then she waved her companion over to pay the bill.

The woman continued to posture while the man paid. As they exited the door, she made it clear she was not done berating him, "I can't believe you left a tip!" the woman said. "She spent nearly two hours on my hair and nails when it shouldn't have taken more than an hour-and-forty-five minutes!"

The man shrugged his shoulders, "I think she made you look really nice."

Having seen her a couple of hours earlier out at the cemetery Agatha had to agree. Whoever did her hair had done a fantastic job.

CHAPTER TWENTY

What Agatha Found

WITH THE ROSE thieves right in front of them, there was no place for Agatha and M. Poirot to hide without calling more attention to themselves. Agatha picked up the terrier and held him close. He let out a small growl.

"Sampson!" She scolded.

M. Poirot gave her another perplexed look.

Agatha went back to pretending to study the list of services offered as the rose thieves and would-be dognappers argued just two feet from where she stood.

"So you're saying I don't always look nice?" the woman said.

"No, that's not what I'm saying." The man had his hands in his pockets, and he seemed to be looking for something. "You look nice. That's what I was saying." He stopped for a moment. "I can't find the keys."

"What do you mean you can't find the keys?"

"I thought what I said was self-explanatory. I'll go check in the salon and see if I left them there." He turned to go back in, "Now aren't you glad I didn't stiff them on the tip?"

"Hmph," she said.

The woman wanted to argue, but she caught a glimpse of her reflection in the window and was pleased with what she saw. Satisfied that her hair looked good, she held out her hands to admire her nails.

"I really wish I'd had time for that pedicure," she said softly. "Men," she said seemingly to no one, "are always in a hurry."

With one of the rose thieves within arm's reach, Agatha was worried the woman would try to engage in conversation and then recognize both her and M. Poirot, but the man emerged in the nick of time.

"They're not there," he said.

"Who's not there?"

"Not who, what. The keys are what's not there," the man said.

"What do you mean, the keys aren't there. They have to be. Keys don't just get up and walk off!"

"Let's go into this Q-G-A-R-S-T, place," the man said spelling out each letter and pointing to the store across the street. "It's where I dropped off the dog. The keys must be there."

"What is a Q-G-A-R … whatever, and why did you leave the dog there?" she said.

"When we got out of the car, it was the first place he wanted to go. We went in, and the clerk said, 'Hello, M. Poirot.' We got to talking. She said she knew the owner and would take care of him."

"The first place you walk into, and they knew the dog?"

"Not they—she. One person."

"What are the chances that the first person you see would know the dog? That dog must be famous. We should've asked for a ransom or a reward or something," she said.

"He's a dog," the man said, "Dogs aren't famous."

"Yes they are," his companion insisted. "Why there's Rin Tin Tin and Lassie and Clifford!"

"Clifford?"

"Yeah, Clifford," she looked at him like he was an idiot. "The big red dog," she said exasperated.

"He's not a real dog," the man said.

"What do you mean?"

"Clifford, he isn't a real dog. He's a character. In a book."

"If he's not real, then why do you know who he is?"

"All right, he's real," the man said, giving up. "Let's go see if the keys are at this place."

When they reached QGARST, there was a sign in the window that read, "back in fifteen minutes."

"Oh, great!" the woman said. "I could have gotten a pedicure. But you said no we need to go in two hours!"

The man cupped his hand to his forehead and peered into the shop.

"So *why* did you leave the keys here?" his companion said.

"I didn't leave them. They probably fell out of my pocket when I was bringing the dog in." He stopped to look at her, "It's not like he's trained or anything. The only trick he knows is 'run away.'"

M. Poirot overheard the remark and made a low, rumbly growl.

"Did you hear that?" the woman said.

"Hear what?"

"That noise."

"What noise?"

"The one that sounded like the wretched creature that broke my nail." The woman looked at their car, then across the street to the salon, and then straight at Agatha. "I know that awful little dog is here somewhere."

"Hello!" a voice called out. It was Andrea. "I was hoping I'd see you again," she greeted the man. "I had a small emergency to attend to after you left, and on my way out, I noticed your keys on the floor."

"So you found them!" he said.

"I did," she said as she unlocked the door of the thrift store. "Come in!"

Outside the shop, Agatha and M. Poirot moved in closer so they could cover the front door. Inside, Andrea was careful not to turn her back on the two criminals. She had no idea what crimes they were up to, but she knew dognappers could not be good people.

"Here, they are," Andrea said, pretending to retrieve the man's keys from behind the counter.

"Thanks," the man said.

"Look at these!" the woman said fingering a pair of high heels with charm encrusted straps.

"I see 'em," the man said.

"These charms are so cute! Why they might even be lucky!"

"It's a pair of shoes," the man said. "Shoes aren't lucky or unlucky. They're shoes."

"A pair of highly sought after designer shoes," Andrea added. "Are you moving to town or just passing through?"

"Just passing through," the woman said.

"That's unfortunate," Andrea said.

"Why?" the woman asked.

"One of those organizers came through town, and everyone has been going through their closets and bringing their stuff here. We've been getting a lot of really nice designer items like the Louboutins you're looking at"

"How much are they?" the woman said.

"I haven't had a chance to price them yet, but probably around $500."

The woman turned to her companion. "Give me $500."

"I don't have any cash on me," the man said.

"Yes you do," the woman argued.

"No, I don't," the man said. "I spent the last of it at the salon."

"Will you be staying the night?" Andrea asked.

"We're getting ready to leave right now," the man said.

"That's too bad!" Andrea said.

"Why is it too bad?" the woman asked.

"M. Poirot's owner," then Andrea looked both ways and leaned forward as if talking to them in confidence, "is quite well off. I'm sure when she finds out how you saved M. Poirot she'll want to give you a very generous reward. Probably enough to cover the cost of these shoes."

"Oh, no, we couldn't do that," the man said, "it's all in a day's, you know, whatever is in a day, it's in all of that." His companion kicked him.

"I mean," he continued, "It wouldn't be right to take money for rescuing a dog because, dogs are like family. You wouldn't want a reward for finding a kid or a grandma. That would be wrong," he turned to the woman and stared at her very hard.

"If you're sure," Andrea said.

"We're sure, right sweetums?" the man said to his companion.

The rose thief glared at her compatriot. "If you say so," she snarled.

Soon the couple left, and a minute later Agatha and M. Poirot entered the shop.

*   *   *

"If it isn't the unbeatable team of Mata Hari and M. Poirot!" Andrea greeted them.

"Mata Hari?"

"The sunglasses, the hat, and carting M. Poirot around like he's a pocket dog."

Agatha laughed. "Right. We were surveilling the store incognito. I thought you might need coverage."

"Well, that was interesting," Andrea said.

"What was interesting?"

"I tried to get them to stay long enough for me to contact the police so Officer Hughes could get here and arrest them. I suggested to her that there could be a sizable reward, but the guy wasn't biting. If I had been able to get her alone, she would have done it. I don't know, she seems greedy or sleazy or maybe greazy—kind of a combination of the two.

"I wonder if that's why she kicked him in the leg. I couldn't see her face, but the back of her was angry."

"The front of her wasn't much happier than the back, when he told her she couldn't have $500 for these shoes," Andrea said holding up the charm laden heels.

They were interrupted by a loud shriek.

Chapter Twenty-One

Capturing the Rose Thieves

"WHAT WAS THAT?" Andrea asked.

"I don't know."

M. Poirot and his leash trailed after the two women as they ran to the front of the store to see what was the matter. What they saw were the dognappers standing next to the burgundy car, and standing next to the car was Officer Steven Hughes with an electronic device in his hand.

"Is that a Taser?" Agatha asked.

"No," Andrea said. "It's one of those electronic ticket writers the city bought. My friend Roscoe wrote an op-ed about them."

"I want your badge number!" It was the woman who dognapped M. Poirot. She was yelling at Steven. "I'm going to write a letter to ... well, whoever it is you write letters to and they print them in the paper."

"If you keep yelling like this, I can and will arrest you," Steven said.

"Nobody gets arrested for parking tickets," the woman replied, "Why it's against the law!"

"It's not against the law, and when you rack up six tickets in less than a week, you certainly *can* get arrested for parking tickets." Steven turned his attention to the ticket writer, "With all the yelling and rude remarks, I can add resisting arrest to the charges."

"How do you know I'm the one who overparked?" the woman asked.

"Overparked?" Steven said.

The woman stood with her arms folded across her chest. "Yeah. Overparked."

Steven finished typing and pressed a button to dispense the ticket. "Here you go," he said handing it to her.

"I don't want it," She put her hands on her hips and refused to accept it.

"If you didn't want a ticket, you should have moved your car before the two hours was up," Steven said.

"I didn't park here," she pointed to her companion, "he did. Besides, the car's a rental."

"If you read your rental agreement, you'll find you're responsible for any parking citations you get while you have the car." Steven placed the ticket under the passenger side windshield wiper.

"You can't put that on my car," the woman said. "First, you cannot touch my car. That is against the law. Second, I already have lots of these," she said, waving her hand at the ticket. "I should arrest you for littering!"

The man stood with his hands in his pockets, looking at a spot on the ground while the woman glared at him.

"Aren't you going to do something?" she said.

"He is doing something," Steven said, "It's called cooperating."

"He's not cooperating. He's standing with his hands in his pockets not saying anything because he doesn't want you to find out…." A flash of realization swept across her face, and she abruptly stopped talking.

The man dropped his head further and looked like he wanted to sink into the ground.

"Find out what?" Steven said.

"Never mind." The woman reached into her purse, pulled out a compact, and freshened her lipstick. Then she looked at Steven. "Okay, you can arrest me. I'm ready for my headshot."

"It's called a mug shot," her companion corrected.

"Mug shot, headshot, it's all the same," she said. "There was this guy who got a big modeling contract from his headshots when he got arrested. Why he even married an heiress."

Back at QGARST, Agatha, Andrea, and M. Poirot were riveted by the scene unfolding in front of them.

"What do you suppose she meant when she said 'he doesn't want you to find out?' Do you think she meant the dognapping?" Andrea asked.

"I don't know," Agatha said, "but if it weren't illegal to gamble, I'd bet this is the first time Steven had a suspect go from resisting arrest to demanding it."

"We'd better let him know that these two are the dognappers. I'm not sure the parking ticket charges will be enough to hold them for fifteen minutes let alone overnight," Andrea said.

Agatha and Andrea were hurrying to tell Steven about the couple when Lynette walked into QGARST.

"I need to talk to you, Andrea."

"Sorry Lynette, I need to report a crime."

"Not so fast," Lynette stood in the doorway and blocked their exit. "You and Agatha have been conspiring against me, and I am going to tell the board of directors."

"This will have to wait, Lynette," Andrea said, "and if you don't get out of my way, I'm going to ask Officer Hughes to arrest you on charges of false imprisonment."

At the mention of Steven's name, Lynette stepped out of the doorway.

"Officer Hughes," Andrea called out, "that's the man!" She pointed at the woman's companion.

"What man?" Steven asked.

"The man who brought M. Poirot into QGARST!" Andrea said. "He's the dognapper."

"He is not," his companion argued. The man pushed his hands deeper into his pockets. He clearly didn't like the direction things were going, and he took a break from looking down at the ground to look up at the sky.

"Yes he is," Andrea insisted.

"What makes you think so?" the woman challenged.

"He walked into QGARST with M. Poirot."

"And that makes him a dognapper?" the woman asked.

"How else would he have gotten the dog?"

The woman pointed to Agatha. "That woman left him at the cemetery."

"What woman?" Steven asked.

"That woman with the bicycle. The one who can't mind her own business."

"Do you mean, Agatha?" Steven asked.

"I don't know. It's not like I run up to every creep and ask their name, but she's been stalking us."

"She's been stalking you?" Steven said doubtfully.

"Yes she has," the woman continued. "The other day when we got to town, she was out at the cemetery, and she turned right in front of our car with that dog in the basket! A couple of days later we were over by that Mrs. Bailey's house, and there she was again. She even tried to chase us on her bicycle! Then today she was just sitting on the gazebo out in the middle of the cemetery not paying a bit of attention to the dog. He got so bored he ran away from her and jumped into my arms!"

"I have not been stalking you," Agatha said confronting the dognappers. "You've been on a two-person crime spree all through Madison County. I saw the way you parked at the assisted living. You took up four parking spaces! And today you took M. Poirot!" Agatha held the terrier in her arms.

"I did not 'take' him!" the woman said. "He attacked me and tried to grab the roses right out of my hand!"

"What roses?" Steven had switched from the handheld ticket writer to a digital notebook the police department was testing.

"The roses that we were taking out to my Aunt Minnie's grave."

"Who is Aunt Minnie, and where is she buried?" It was clear to Steven this was not an ordinary parking violation.

"He said he was here to pay his respects to his father's Granduncle Gottlieb!" Andrea said pointing to the woman's companion.

"It seems to me, one of you must be lying," Steven said looking at the man and the woman.

"Or both of them," offered Agatha, "the only grave they were visiting today was Arnold Brown's, and she wasn't leaving roses, she was taking them!"

"I told you she was stalking us!" the woman said as she pointed a freshly manicured finger toward Agatha. "Arrest her!"

"You took roses from a grave?" Steven said, entering the information into the digital notebook. "What time was this?"

"What does it matter what time it was? It's not like it's illegal," the woman said, "The real crime is letting all of those beautiful flowers go to waste. If you don't salvage them, they wilt to death. I was just trying to rescue them. If you do to an animal what people do to flowers, you can go to jail!"

"Can you please stop talking?" The man had not spoken in so long everyone had forgotten he was there. "You are going to get us in so much trouble. I told you we should leave after breakfast." Then he looked at Steven. "Which way to the police station?"

"I can't arrest you without cause," Steven said.

"Then arrest me for the parking tickets the way you said you would," the man suggested.

"You want me to arrest you for the parking tickets?" Steven asked.

"Please just book me so I can post bail," the man said.

"Hey, you said you didn't have any money!" the woman yelled.

The man shoved his hands deeper into his pockets.

"If you had just given me the money you're going to use to post bail, I could've bought those shoes, and we wouldn't be in this mess!"

"How do you figure that?" the man sneered.

"Those shoes were loaded with lucky charms. If you had given me the money to buy them, we wouldn't have gotten another ticket, and this would never have happened."

"It's not my fault," the man countered. "I told you we shouldn't take that headstone. It's brought us nothing but bad luck! And look," he said pointing at the car, "the back tires are so low we couldn't make a clean getaway if we tried!"

"But that headstone has my name on it!"

"It says 'Let roses bloom and willows wave.' Your name is 'Rose,' not roses!"

The woman burst into tears. Then she pulled out a compact. "Look at me!" she said, mascara running down her face. "This headshot was supposed to be my big chance."

"Agatha, I'll see you at the police station," Steven said. "You'll need to give a statement to Detective Lee while I book these two."

Before heading to the police station, Agatha and M. Poirot made a detour to QGARST with Andrea.

"I know you need to get started with your crochet design," Andrea said handing Agatha a beat up crochet hook and ball of bright pink yarn. "This came in the other day, and I thought you might be able to use it."

"Thanks," Agatha said, and with that, she and M. Poirot were out the door.

When they arrived at the police station they were ushered into a room with a door and a two-way mirror. Agatha took out the hook and yarn to calm herself. Soon a pleasant looking young woman named Detective Lee joined them. Agatha had the unsettling sense that she had seen her before, but where?

"We haven't met, have we?" Agatha asked.

"No," the detective said, "I don't always remember names, but I never forget a face, and I would definitely have remembered this cutie." Detective Lee scratched M. Poirot under his chin. He enjoyed it so much, he raised his muzzle so she could more easily pet him.

"He's my mom's dog," Agatha offered. "His name is M. Poirot."

"Oh, he's a detective like me!" she said brightly. Her face suddenly turned somber, "So why are you two here?"

M. Poirot sat on Agatha's lap as she told the detective the saga of the previous week and her encounters with the rose thieves.

"Is that everything?"

Agatha thought for a moment. "There is one more thing," she said, "I'm working on a crochet design, and I went to visit a woman named Abigail Rowen...."

The detective looked up, startled. "You don't mean the Abigail Rowen who lives at Quercus Grove Assisted Living Center, do you?"

"Yes, that's the one," Agatha continued, "I was there to talk to her about a cloche I bought from QGARST. I had been told that if anyone knew anything about the hat it was Abigail. While we were talking, that couple drove into the parking lot, and," Agatha leaned in, "Abigail said she had seen them the day before when her niece...."

"...took her out to the cemetery," the detective said, finishing Agatha's sentence.

"Yes." Agatha's blood ran cold. How did the detective know what Abigail told her?

"I'm the niece."

"Oh," Agatha said. "You're the young woman whose photo is in Abigail's shadow box! That's why you look familiar." The two women laughed.

Agatha thanked Detective Lee and, with a firm grip on M. Poirot, stood up to leave.

The strip of bright pink stitches she made spilled from her lap onto the floor. With a clank the hook landed under a chair, while the ball of yarn rolled under the table to the most distant corner of the room.

"Let me help," Detective Lee offered. She retrieved the hook, then crossed the room to get the yarn. She rewound it as she made her way back to Agatha.

"Thank you," Agatha said. "It's been a very long day."

There was the agricultural espionage assignment, Mrs. Bailey nearly stumbling onto Agatha's discoveries about William Dettmer, M. Poirot's dognapping, and the long ride home.

And that was just the beginning.

Complicating things further was the fact she had not made a single stitch's worth of progress toward the hat design she needed to finish in just forty-eight hours. Agatha surveyed the long strip of double crochet stitches she made during the interview with Detective Lee and wondered how she would get everything done.

CHAPTER TWENTY-TWO

What the Wills Revealed

"**H**OLD YOUR HORSES!" Agatha said.

After a long day M. Poirot was in a hurry to get home, and in his hurry, he had gotten tangled up in the ball of yarn attached to the long trail of stitches Agatha made.

She set him in the bicycle basket as she sorted out the mess.

"Arf," M. Poirot barked sharply.

"Stop that," Agatha replied.

After the day's events, she wasn't about to let him off his leash even though it would, in theory, make the task easier. She felt his angry, impatient breath on her hands as she untangled the yarn careful not to pull out any stitches.

Then, several deft under and over moves later, the crochet and the dog were separated. "Happy?" She asked as she secured M. Poirot in his seat.

He gave a growl of what sounded like approval.

Agatha sighed with relief. In her wildest nightmares, she never imagined she could feel grateful to see M. Poirot, but after losing him to the dognappers and making the five-mile trek back to town with no hope of finding him, she *was* glad to see him. In fact, she was very glad. She had not known she could feel such joy at seeing another being who loathed her so thoroughly.

The two of them were about to head over to the gas station to put air in her tires, when Lynette appeared.

"I can hold that for you," Lynette offered, pointing to Agatha's crochet bag—the one with the wills she needed to read. The offer to help was uncharacteristically friendly, but then everything about the day had been strange.

"Thanks, but I've got it," Agatha said patting the side of the bag to reassure herself the documents were still there.

"Andrea chewed me out when she got back to QGARST," Lynette confessed. "She said those rose thieves kidnapped M. Poirot, and they had been stalking my mother. I really shouldn't have yelled at you."

"It's been kind of crazy," Agatha said, not wanting to ignore or acknowledge Lynette's attempt at an apology. "I didn't know there was a black market for roses."

"Me either," said Lynette.

They walked a block and a half in silence before reaching the corner of Main and Union.

"I'm going to the gas station," Agatha said trying to ditch her new BFF. "I need to put air in my tires."

"I'm headed that way, too," Lynette said. "I need to get my mom a Violet Crumble."

"Is that a kind of rose?" Agatha asked.

"It's a candy bar. The gas station is the only place in town that carries them. She asked me to get one after I finished my errands," Lynette paused. "She's probably wondering why I'm late. I was supposed to be home by four o'clock to walk Peaches."

"I'm sure she'll understand," Agatha said.

"Maybe," Lynette replied, unconvinced. "You know, I always thought of my mother's roses as a 'hobby.' I didn't know that there were rose thieves who would spy on her and try to steal her roses. Why she could have been kidnapped or even killed!"

They continued their trek to the gas station chatting about the success of the Chocolate & Coffee Festival and Mrs. Bailey's plans to start an heirloom rose festival. "I guess this whole chocolate and coffee thing inspired her," Lynette said.

"It has been kind of fun," Agatha said. "You know, when it's not dangerous."

"Yeah," Lynette agreed.

When they reached the gas station, Lynette went to buy the candy bar, and Agatha and M. Poirot made a beeline for the air compressor.

With her tires properly inflated, Agatha could have continued the day's bicycling adventures, but she decided to take it slow and push M. Poirot and her bike the rest of the way home.

"That was a narrow escape," she whispered to M. Poirot. "It might not have gone as well if Lynette found out about the documents I printed this morning. And no matter what she says, I know she's still mad about the hat."

Agatha was surprised to catch herself talking to the dog. She really was becoming and old lady.

When they finally got home, M. Poirot let out a yelp of relief.

"I hear you," she said as she opened the door. "Today was quite an adventure." Agatha set the crochet tote on the dining table and made her way to the kitchen. "I don't know about you," she said to M. Poirot, "but I want dinner. Then I need to sit down and read."

The dog's ears perked up at the word "dinner."

Agatha could not see what was going on in his doggy head, but she imagined he was thinking of a pork chop with the meat falling off the bone and a side of sweet potato. No doubt he would find the chicken and rice she was serving a bit boring, but he wouldn't be nearly as disappointed as she would be if there weren't any clue about a living relation to Amelia somewhere in the documents she had printed out.

When he heard the ding of the microwave M. Poirot ran into the kitchen ready to eat. Meanwhile, Agatha made a peanut butter and jelly sandwich and thought about the day's events.

After a full day of intrigue, research, espionage, surveillance, and a dognapping, she was ready for a nap, but sleep would have to wait. She needed to find a living heir to Amelia Dettmer.

Relation. She was simply looking for a relation. A living one.

With dinner done Agatha made a fresh pot of coffee and sat down at the kitchen table to read all 217 pages of the probate records.

She pulled the stack of papers from the crochet bag. The clerk had thoughtfully arranged the documents in reverse chronological order, so William Dettmer's will was right on top. Written eight weeks before his death, Agatha learned William had been married twice. His first wife—Clara Davis Dettmer of Liberty Prairie—had died years earlier. In addition to Amelia, the will mentioned an adult child from his first marriage — a son named Samuel Dettmer.

What, Agatha wondered, had become of Amelia's half-brother, Samuel?

Using the rudimentary family tree she pieced together from William Dettmer's will, Agatha made her way to the dining table and turned on her computer to search for any available online records.

Her first stop was a website with free access to census and death records, which in turn led her to a website that specialized in documenting cemeteries. It was there she found an image of a headstone for William Dettmer's first wife, Clara. She was buried in Liberty Prairie Cemetery alongside her parents.

Next Agatha found an image of the headstone Steven Hughes pulled from the car of the rose thieves just a few hours earlier — Minnie Dettmer — beloved daughter of Friedrich and Dorthea Dettmer. Who, she wondered, were Friedrich and Dorthea?

Having exhausted all of her leads at the genealogy websites, Agatha's next stop was QGPL.org, where she could access Quercus Grove Public Library's online resources which included a searchable database of more than a century of *The Acorn Register*. Unable to find what she was looking for, Agatha broke down and texted her friend, Hank.

"How do I access the online archives of *The Acorn* from my library account?" Agatha watched the screen of her phone for signs of life. First there was nothing. Then the screen lit up with moving dots in a bubble of would-be words. Then more nothing. Finally words appeared.

"Why do you want to access *The Acorn*?"

"I'm working on the Amelia Dettmer case."

Nothing, nothing, and more nothing. Agatha went back to searching the land records she could reach through the county recorder's website. She was about to read over an interesting deed when her phone pinged.

"What are you trying to find?"

"Amelia Dettmer's relatives."

Then there were lots of dots followed by a long message.

"First, log into your library account. Once you are in, click on the upper right hand corner where it says 'Special Online Collections.'"

But Agatha only got as far as logging in when a message appeared: FAILURE TO RETURN BORROWED ITEM(S) HAS RESULTED IN YOUR QGPL ACCOUNT BEING FROZEN. PLEASE RETURN THE OVERDUE ITEM(S) AND MEET WITH A LIBRARIAN TO HAVE THIS FREEZE LIFTED.

"I had trouble logging in," Agatha texted back.

"What kind of trouble?"

"I got a message in all caps that my account had been frozen."

"You must have something overdue."

"But I've only checked out one item, and that was just a little over a week ago," Agatha said.

"What about that interlibrary loan you picked up? Have you returned that?" Hank asked.

"No, but it hasn't been two weeks."

"Interlibrary loans are only one week."

"Oh." Agatha could think of nothing to say.

"If you return the book first thing in the morning, I can clear your account, and you can access the records," Hank offered.

"But I need to do the research tonight."

Agatha's phone went dark.

Then it rang.

It was Hank. "Tell me what you're looking for," she said with an air of resignation and curiosity. "I'll log into my account, and we'll see if we can find it."

For several hours, Agatha read over genealogy and county records she could see and directed Hank to dates of interest at the QGPL online archives of *The Acorn*.

Agatha heard the town clock strike ten just as Hank unearthed an obituary for William Dettmer's first wife. It covered the highlights of her life, referencing the year she married William Dettmer, and the birth of not one but two sons: Samuel, whom Agatha had learned about earlier in the evening, and Matthias, a younger son she had not known existed.

The widower Dettmer found himself with two young children to raise, a situation he remedied by marrying Miss Emma Phillips. *The Acorn Register* reported that the new Mr. and Mrs. Dettmer were joined in matrimony in a courthouse ceremony with his sister, Minnie Dettmer, and family friend, Sevilla Bartlett, as witnesses.

With these new pieces of the puzzle, Agatha now knew that Minnie was William's sister, and Friedrich, and Dorthea were the parents of them both. She also had the learned the mysterious Sevilla's full name.

And that was all *The Acorn* deemed newsworthy for most of the next thirteen years. Then, in the spring of 1915, there was a notice of the birth of "baby girl Dettmer" on May 7. A few weeks later, there was a brief mention of the christening of Miss Amelia Dettmer, daughter of Mr. and Mrs. William Dettmer.

The Dettmers didn't appear in *The Acorn* again until 1917. First was a death notice for Matthias where it was reported he died as the result of an artillery malfunction while training in Fort Riley, Kansas. Three days later, an obituary was published noting that he left behind his father, his step-mother, his brother, Samuel, and his half-sister Amelia.

After that the sorrows would not stop.

In January 1919, *The Acorn* reported that Amelia's mother, Emma, had gone to Nebraska. Eight weeks later, there was an obituary for Amelia's mother who had taken ill with the flu while caring for an elderly aunt. Amelia's mother's remains were interred in a family plot in Broken Bow, Nebraska beside her aunt.

Back in Quercus Grove, the ink was barely dry on Emma's probate records when Amelia's father, William, drowned while swimming in a river in Hawaii where he had gone to visit his son Samuel. Amelia was now all alone in the world save for the mysterious Sevilla Bartlett who, Agatha learned from census records, stepped in to raise her.

"It's getting kind of late," Hank said, yawning.

"Wow," Agatha said, looking at the time on her computer screen, "I'd better let you go before your carriage turns into a pumpkin!"

Agatha said good-bye then started to organize the articles Hank had sent her. She had just finished work on Amelia's family tree when M. Poirot awoke with a start—the result of a doggy nightmare brought on, no doubt, by the day's misadventures.

Agatha took a break from her research to fix him a snack. While he ate, she sat at the kitchen table and studied the cloche. If she could just find the code maybe she could solve the case of

Amelia Dettmer, but she could barely hear herself think with the terrier's noisy eating.

"Really, M. Poirot, do you have to be so loud?"— chomp chomp, chomp CRUNCH CRUNCH chomp CRUNCH CRUNCH chomp CRUNCH, chomp CRUNCH CRUNCH chomp chomp chomp.

Agatha shook her head. She could have sworn M. Poirot had just spelled out "I want pie," in Morse Code. She definitely needed to sleep.

But she needed to find a living relation to Amelia Dettmer even more. She examined the hat again, and while she was pretty sure M. Poirot did not know Morse Code, it seemed that Sevilla Bartlett did. As Agatha looked at the stitching that Lynette said made the hat "too busy," she decoded a message.

"Happy twenty-first birthday to one of a kind and the last of a kind. May fortune and goodwill follow you all of your days."

CHAPTER TWENTY-THREE

Looking for a Lost Relation

T HE NEXT MORNING, Agatha awoke to hot doggy breath. M. Poirot had vaulted onto her bed and was licking her face in an attempt to bring her back to life. As the world slowly came into focus she looked at the clock by her bed and saw that it was already 9:07.

She had twenty-three minutes to get herself and M. Poirot ready for a meeting with Marcus before he was due in court. There was so much to tell him.

It had been a long but productive night, and Agatha was sure she had found a living relation to Amelia Dettmer. Thanks to Hank searching for and reading through dozens of articles in the online database of *The Acorn* archives, Agatha was able to flesh out the life of Amelia Dettmer and fill in her family tree.

A tree that included her mother and father—both of whom were Pioneers of Quercus Grove—and two half-brothers who had been lost to time.

Then there were the Pioneers of Quercus Grove applications. The information on the USB stick her mother foisted on her as she flitted off to Istanbul turned out to be a digital gold mine.

Using the search function, Agatha had identified a subset of pioneers who had banded together to secure the future of any "spinsters" who might descend from them. It would have taken months to find everything she needed if she'd had to sort through the papers. Instead, after one incredibly long night, she had figured it out.

And now she needed to see Marcus.

Agatha and M. Poirot were ready in record time, making it to Marcus's office with two minutes to spare. Armed with the wills she printed out at the Clerk of Court, the notes she made while on the phone with Hank, and the information she unearthed in the pioneers applications, Agatha laid out her findings.

"So, Amelia Dettmer has a living relation by the name of Samantha Russell?" Marcus said.

"Yes" Agatha said. "Of course, I was running on caffeine fumes for the last couple of hours, but she is the great great granddaughter of Amelia's half-brother, Matthias. At the time of his death, no one knew that he was married and his wife was pregnant."

"And what about this trust?"

"It was set up by some of the original pioneers of Quercus Grove when the settlement attained village status. If an unmarried adult female was certified to be a Pioneer of Quercus

Grove on both sides of her family, she was eligible to receive an annual stipend. Amelia was the last eligible descendant."

"That is certainly interesting."

"There is one more bit that is even more interesting."

"What is it?"

"Mr. Bailey has been collecting money from the trust since Lynette turned twenty-one."

"But you said Amelia was the last eligible recipient."

"Yes, I did."

"If you're right, then…."

"Then maybe a document was forged to gain access to the trust. And then maybe a certain elderly neighbor was being harassed by the forger, and she found out and told him she would expose him if he didn't leave her alone and let her have her Lusitania Day celebrations."

"Maybe," Marcus agreed.

"I emailed the spreadsheet to you. It has all of my comments with links and citations to pertinent documents and articles."

"Thank you," Marcus said, "I'll have to read through it after I get out of court this afternoon. I don't think Thomas Bailey will be very happy his secret has been uncovered. I can't imagine what Lynette will do with the news." He paused. "I wonder how she will remake herself?"

"I don't have time to wonder," Agatha said. "I misplaced a library book I borrowed, and now it's overdue. The only reason I was able to get this done last night was that Hank logged into her account and looked up everything in the online database of *The Acorn Register*." She paused for a moment. "Now that this is almost wrapped up, I need to get back to work on that hat design. It needs to be in the mail tomorrow morning."

"Thanks for the report," Marcus said. "If I have any questions, I'll get back to you."

As Agatha and M. Poirot headed out of Marcus's office, her thoughts were all awhirl. She knew she needed to find the design book she checked out and concentrate on making the hat, but she didn't think a latte would hurt. "What do you say, M. Poirot? Shall we stop at The Coffee Shop?"

After the hubbub of the Chocolate & Coffee Festival, The Coffee Shop, which was busy, seemed almost deserted by comparison.

"You're just the person I wanted to see," Sam greeted her.

"And you're just the person I wanted to see," Agatha said enthusiastically.

"You left this here," she said handing Agatha the missing library book. "I meant to take it by your house the other day, but it's been crazy here."

"No kidding," Agatha said. With the missing book having magically reappeared, she now had one item off of her too-long to-do list. "You saved my bacon," she said to Sam.

Then Agatha opened the book that was nearly her undoing. She read through the page titled CONTENTS. After not finding what she was looking for, she turned to the EXTENDED CONTENTS and read through that until she reached "Chapter 14: Various accessories." She was about turn to "The Millinery Workroom" on page 260 when a voice interrupted.

"If you're not going to place an order, can you let me go ahead?" It was Lynette, and she seemed to be feeling more herself after a good night's rest.

"Sure," Agatha said. She knew changes were in store for Lynette, and figured a strong cup of coffee couldn't hurt.

Lynette's eyes narrowed. "Why are you being so nice?"

"I'm not being 'so' nice," Agatha said.

Lynette gave Agatha a side-eye death stare. "You know you could just place your order. This is a coffee shop, not a library. Some of us have things to do!"

"Well, then order your coffee and go do them," Agatha said, wondering if the things Lynette needed to do involved trying to bury the truth about Amelia Dettmer.

Still Lynette stayed glued to the floor in her place in line behind Agatha.

"No, really. Go ahead," Agatha said.

With some misgiving, Lynette finally took the place in front of Agatha and ordered.

"I'll have a caramel mocha cappuccino, with soy milk," she paused. "Make that with oat milk."

Sam, a ninja master of patience, waited while Lynette went through her order permutations: what she thought she should drink, what seemed like a viable compromise between what she thought she should drink and what she wanted, and finally ordering what she wanted.

"Never mind. Make it with whole milk. Please." Then she set her money on the counter.

Sam made the cappuccino with two foam hearts ensconced in swirls of caramel.

"Oh, no," Lynette said. "It's too pretty to drink!"

"Come back tomorrow, and I'll make you another one," Sam said.

"I'll have a 16-ounce whole milk latte with an extra shot."

"Not a 12-ounce cappuccino?" Sam asked, smiling.

"Not today, I need the extra caffeine.... It was a long night," she added.

"Celebrating?" It took a moment for Agatha to place the somewhat familiar voice. It was "Adam" or whatever his name was.

"Celebrating what?" she said.

"The capture of Bonnie and Clyde," he pointed to the headline of *The Acorn Register:* DOGNAPPING ROSE THIEVESS-ESCAPE THWARTED!

Agatha began reading the article.

> In a page that could have been ripped from a novel by the famed detection writer, Agatha Christie, Quercus Grove's own Agatha Christine — with the help of her mother's dog, the aptly named, M. Poirot — foiled two hardened criminals intent on stealing Katharine Bailey's famed roses and Minnie Dettmer's headstone!

"Thanks for the help," he said, handing her his card. "If you're ever in a jam, call me."

"Okay," Agatha said in between sips of coffee. She looked at his card. His name really was Adam. Adam Goodman, and he was a federal agent. She put his card in her wallet and hoped she would never need to take him up on the offer.

With a living relation for Amelia Dettmer identified, the book she didn't know she had misplaced found, and the rose thieves behind bars, Agatha had one thing left to do: design a crochet hat, and she had 24 hours to do it.

"Let's go," she said to M. Poirot.

He looked at Agatha with consternation. Usually he had to prod her to leave The Coffee Shop.

Agatha took M. Poirot straight home. After a morning filled with adventure, they ate a late breakfast and a took an even later walk. Then M. Poirot, exhausted by the previous 24 hours, settled in for a long nap while Agatha sat down to design a hat.

She looked at the hats featured in the overdue library book that nearly thwarted her efforts to find a living relation to Amelia and then back at the cloche she had purchased at QGARST. The bell of the hat was worked in a single, long horsehair strip rather than the single piece in-the-round increases crochet cloches were typically worked in.

Agatha listened with envy as M. Poirot softly snored. After doing what felt like a lot of nothing, she took the chain of stitches she had made at the police station and held it up against the hat. The foundation double crochet she had been practicing was almost exactly the same width as the horsehair strip used to make the cloche she had purchased at QGARST.

The strip was more flexible than a standard double crochet foundation, and it curved in one direction, but Agatha was certain something could be done with it. It suddenly hit her that she might have figured out a solution. Using more than a dozen removable stitch markers, she fashioned the bright pink crochet strip into a cloche.

It didn't go well.

There were gaps, the transitions weren't smooth, but when she put it on her head, as imperfect as it was, it had all of the elements of something that could be special. If only she had a Styrofoam head like the ones in the window of the Cutting Edge!

Agatha looked at the clock. It was quarter to five.

Where had the day gone?

With no time to waste, she got online and searched for "styrofoam heads near me."

According to the search results, the nearest Styrofoam head was at a beauty supply store four miles away as the crow flies. Agatha's problem was that she wasn't a crow, and the ride over surface streets was five miles. The beauty supply store would be closed before she got there.

The next nearest Styrofoam head was at a craft store in the next town over. Even if she had the time, which she didn't, her legs were too tired from the previous day's adventure to make the trek.

I need something that's actually near me, Agatha thought. Then she remembered that QGARST used Styrofoam heads to display the hats that came in. The thrift closed at 4:30, but maybe Andrea hadn't left yet and would let her borrow one.

She dialed the number. One ring, two rings, three rings, and then the call went to voicemail.

Agatha was about to give up when she remembered seeing several Styrofoam heads in the display case of the salon where the rose thief went to get her broken nail fixed, and they didn't close until six. She looked up the number and called. One ring, two rings, then someone picked up.

"Cutting Edge, this is Lauren. How can I help you?"

"My name is Agatha Bigelow, and I was wondering if I could buy one of the Styrofoam heads you have in the window."

"You want to buy a Styrofoam head?"

"Yes, I'm trying to finish…"

Lauren cut her off, "We don't sell ours, but you can buy them at the beauty supply store."

"The beauty supply place is only open for another twelve minutes, and I don't have time to get there before they close," Agatha said.

"Oh, wait," the stylist said, suddenly animated, "Are you Agatha Christine?"

"Yes," Agatha said warily.

"The Agatha Christine with the orange bicycle and the dog who captured the rose thieves?"

"Yes," Agatha said, unsure how to respond to her newfound celebrity.

"That story is all anyone was talking about today. How long would it take you to get here?"

"Ten minutes," Agatha said.

"Great," Lauren replied, "and if you can, bring M. Poirot, with you!"

Agatha roused the terrier from his nap, "We need to pick up a Styrofoam head," she explained.

"Grrr," he replied.

In no time they were at the salon. Lauren and several other stylists and customers oohed and aahed over M. Poirot. "He's such a hero," said one.

"And so brave," said another.

M. Poirot lapped up the attention while Lauren put the Styrofoam head in a bag for Agatha to take home.

"So why do you need this?" she asked, politely feigning interest.

"I'm working on a hat design."

"Good luck!" Lauren said then returned to visiting with M. Poirot.

Yes, Agatha thought, I could certainly use some luck.

CHAPTER TWENTY-FOUR

The Coup de Grace

"**M**ARCUS, IT'S ALMOST two o'clock. Everyone should be here in a few minutes," Agatha said. "I can hardly wait!"

It was like the denouement of a decluttering show when everyone meets up to see the "big reveal." Agatha took one last look at the arrangement. She wanted a good view of all the parties so she could watch their expressions as events unfolded.

"I can't tell what you're more excited about: saving QGARST, or the thrill of solving the mystery," Marcus said.

"I think it's saving QGARST," then Agatha paused. "But it was a very intriguing mystery." She moved a potted fern that interfered with one of her lines of sight. "Won't everyone be surprised? Especially the Baileys. Do you think they'll come?"

"I'm sure the Baileys will be here, and if they're smart they will bring outside counsel with them. As soon as they learn it's been discovered they violated the terms of the Quercus Grove

Pioneer Trust, they would be well-advised to say nothing. It remains to be seen if they are able to follow that advice. As soon as you outbid Lynette on the cloche, her father must have worried you would unravel the secret."

"Are you sure they violated the terms of the trust?" Agatha asked.

"I'm sure," Marcus said. "I've gone over it carefully, and as far as I can tell, they violated the terms of the trust, and they did so knowingly. Amelia Dettmer was peculiar, but she was nobody's fool. The repercussions of this will echo far outside the walls of this office once the truth is known."

"It's too bad Amelia couldn't be here for this day," Agatha said. "It's clear she wanted the wrongdoers exposed."

"It will probably be a great surprise to everyone but the Baileys," the attorney said with a smile. "Settling this estate might have taken years without your work. I have to thank you, Agatha."

"You're welcome, Marcus. You know I love a good mystery," Agatha said, smiling. "That and I can hardly wait to see the look on Lynette's face."

"There may be awkward moments with the Baileys," Marcus cautioned.

"There are always awkward moments with the Baileys, and this time, you can't blame them. A lot of people don't want to lose their social standing."

"We'll see what happens," said Marcus.

Agatha looked out the window. "Sam is coming up the walk, and she's brought Andrea with her!" she said. "I'm dying to tell them the news."

"FRONT DOOR OPEN," the alarm system announced the arrival of Sam and Andrea.

Agatha also welcomed them and made sure they got the most comfortable seats with the second best view the conference room had to offer.

"Is it true a relation to Amelia Dettmer has been found?" Andrea asked.

"You and all of Quercus Grove will know shortly," Agatha said.

As soon as they were seated, the alarm signaled that more people had entered the office. This time it was the president and treasurer of the board of QGARST dressed in their "doing business for QGARST suits"—one houndstooth and one navy. A few minutes later the secretary for the Quercus Grove Historical Museum & Society arrived with a small rolling suitcase. "Will you be staying with us long?" Agatha teased.

"It looks like every one is here now except the Baileys," Marcus commented. "We should wait until they are here before we start. No doubt they will have a number of questions and possibly an objection or two."

Just then, the alarm sounded FRONT DOOR OPEN and the Baileys—along with a woman in a tailored black pantsuit who looked like she might be the attorney Marcus thought they should bring with them—walked through the door.

"What is the point of this meeting?" Mr. Bailey demanded, "You know as well as I that Amelia Dettmer has no 'heir.' She died all alone in the world, and any claim that she had an heir is false!"

"Why don't you join us in the conference room," Marcus suggested.

"This looks like a conspiracy to me," Lynette said.

"You might be right about a conspiracy, but you might not be right about who it involves," Marcus cautioned.

Lynette's face reddened.

Meanwhile, Mr. Bailey quietly conferred with the woman who had come with them.

"If you and your guest will be seated, Mr. Bailey, I will explain how a living relation to Amelia Dettmer was identified. Of course," Marcus continued, "a DNA test will be necessary to confirm the paper record."

"Hmpf," Mr. Bailey said.

With everyone seated, and the faces of all parties visible to Agatha, Marcus began the presentation.

"As you are aware from the reporting done by *The Acorn Register* when Amelia Dettmer died, there was a condition to her will that a search for *a living relation* be conducted, and if *a living relation*—again, I am using her words—were found, the bulk of the estate would go to Quercus Grove Animal Shelter Rescue and Thrift, also known as QGARST. The remainder would go to the Quercus Grove Historical Museum & Society."

What was not reported is that Amelia Dettmer was a descendant of a small group of Quercus Grove Pioneers who had set up a special trust to take care of their unmarried daughters. Amelia Dettmer was the last living person eligible to receive moneys from this trust.

"I will now lay out the results of the research that was done to find a living relation to Amelia Dettmer. This draws on land records, probate records, Quercus Grove Pioneer applications, and items from the archives of *The Acorn Register*.

"As I think most of us know, Amelia Dettmer was born right here in Quercus Grove, as were her parents and all of her parents' parents."

He turned to the secretary of the Quercus Grove Historical Museum & Society. "Both Amelia's mother and father were certified Pioneers of Quercus Grove. Is that not correct?"

"That is correct," the secretary said.

"And did you bring documentation of that?" Marcus asked.

"I did," she said placing two large navy blue binders on the table.

Marcus continued. "In addition to being a Pioneer of Quercus Grove on both sides of the family going back to the founding of our great village, Amelia Dettmer was devoted to the welfare of the animals of Quercus Grove and the surrounding county of Madison, is that not correct?"

This time Marcus turned his gaze toward the president and treasurer of QGARST who looked at each other and nodded their heads in agreement. "That is correct," the president said.

"This isn't news," Mr. Bailey said dismissively.

"Yeah, it's not news," Lynette said echoing her father's words.

"So we can agree, at least in theory," Marcus said, "that Amelia Dettmer had every reason to want to do what she could to improve both Quercus Grove, where she was raised, and Madison County, where her last home was located. To the best of my knowledge, Madison County is the only place Amelia Dettmer ever resided, and the place was in her blood, so to speak."

At this part of the speech, Mr. Bailey looked uncomfortable, and he gave Lynette a side-eye glance. "I don't know what agreeing or disagreeing to that adds to the discussion," Mr.

Bailey said. The woman who came with the Baileys passed a note to Mr. Bailey.

"I'm sorry, Ms., I didn't catch your name or in what capacity you are here," Marcus said.

"Yes. I'm Karen Wheeler, and I'm an attorney."

"Really?" Marcus raised his eyebrows, "Do you mind if I ask what kind of law you practice?"

Karen Wheeler coughed, "I'm just here as a friend of the family today."

Marcus persisted, "Are you any relation to the Karen Wheeler who defended the Gang of Seven in federal court?"

"I am that Karen Wheeler," the woman admitted reluctantly.

Marcus looked directly at Mr. Bailey. "She's a good friend to have. I'd listen to any advice she might give you."

Then Marcus resumed his presentation.

"There are, as you know, few people alive today whose roots in Quercus Grove go back as far or as deep as Amelia's did." He waited for one of the Baileys to chime in and argue the point, but they didn't. "Particularly on both sides."

Marcus continued. "One thing you all might wonder is 'how did Amelia survive?' She had no known job, and the only thing she ever seemed to do was pick up stray animals in need of a home and care for them. Often she was able to find them new homes, but those that were harder or impossible to place, she kept."

"Well, I'll tell you," Marcus continued. "Amelia was the beneficiary of a generous trust. One intended for 'spinster' daughters of a select group of the pioneer families of Quercus Grove.

"There was one additional requirement," he said, "and that is that in addition to the recipient having never married, she also had to descend from this group of pioneers on not one but both sides of her family.

"On the occasion of Amelia's twenty-first birthday, she was presented with a hat by another beneficiary of the trust—a Miss Sevilla Bartlett—a world-renowned hat maker.

"Worked into the hat was a coded message which reads: 'Happy twenty-first birthday to one of a kind and the last of a kind. May fortune and goodwill follow you all of your days.'"

"As such, Amelia was the last living person eligible to receive funds from that trust!"

"That can't be right!" Lynette said.

Marcus continued. "I'm afraid that is right, Lynette, and I further assert that you and your father have known that for years, as did Amelia."

"But what we are here to learn today is this: does Amelia Dettmer have a living relation?"

"A living relation is NOT the same thing as an heir," Lynette said pointedly.

"No, Lynette, it's not, but as Amelia was the last living person *entitled* to receive disbursements from the trust, she had the responsibility to identify where the remaining funds should go once she died. She set the condition that if a living relation were found, the money would go to QGARST."

The room fell silent. Finally, Andrea broke the ice. "So who is this living relation? Is it someone in the room?"

"I'm glad you asked," Marcus said, clearly relieved to be able to get back to his presentation. "As a result of all of Agatha's work, we have identified Samantha Russell as Amelia's living relation."

"Me?" Sam said. "How is that possible? I'm not from here."

"You aren't, but your great great granduncle Samuel Dettmer was, and Amelia was his half-sister," Marcus said.

"You mean, the uncle I'm named for was from Quercus Grove?" Sam asked.

"Yes, born and raised. But he moved to Hawaii in search of warmer weather and bigger adventures. After the untimely demise of Emma Dettmer—Amelia's mother—William went to visit Samuel in Hawaii, where he drowned while swimming in a river. Soon after, Samuel left Hawaii and moved to San Francisco where he worked as a welder.

"One day a private detective hired by a woman named Opal Hill Dettmer showed up on his doorstep, and it was then he learned Matthias had married shortly before his fatal accident. His wife was pregnant at the time of his death, and six months later the Widow Dettmer gave birth to a daughter, Mathilda. She would grow up, marry, and have a daughter of her own, Rhonda Paxson Harris who would grow up, marry, and have a daughter of her own Carol Harris Russell who...."

"...is my mother!" Sam said finishing Marcus's sentence.

"The fact that you are a living relation to Amelia Dettmer means that QGARST will now be able to receive the funds that are so desperately needed."

"I don't see what any of this has to do with us," Mrs. Bailey said.

"Unfortunately, Mrs. Bailey, Lynette is not entitled to the funds she has been collecting from the trust," Marcus said, "and it remains to be seen if the remedy will be civil, criminal, or both."

Mrs. Bailey's eyes opened wide with horror. She turned to her husband. "Thomas, is this true?"

"Parts of it might be, but...."

"I'm advising you not to talk," Ms. Wheelser said.

So, on advice of counsel, the Baileys packed up and left. The next to go were the president and treasurer of the board of QGARST, and, after Agatha helped her sort and put away documents, the secretary of the Quercus Grove Historical Museum & Society went on her way.

After a round of thank-yous and good-byes, Andrea and Sam left to celebrate.

So why did Amelia put in the provision of the living relation?" Agatha asked.

"I think she wanted to make sure Mr. Bailey got exposed."

"Will he still be able to practice law?"

"I don't know. We'll have to see."

And with that, Marcus turned out the lights and they each headed home.

CHAPTER TWENTY-FIVE

A Reward

"**H**AVE YOU HEARD about the Baileys?" Lydia asked one morning a couple of months after Sam was revealed to be a living relation to Amelia Dettmer.

Agatha had just returned from a whirlwind tour of fiber festivals after a tremendous reception to her first crochet design.

"No, I haven't," Agatha said hoping she didn't sound like she cared.

Undeterred by her daughter's lack of interest, Lydia continued. "At first it looked like the Baileys would have dire financial problems from the fraud perpetrated on the trust. Then, that new editor of the paper, Rocko...."

"Roscoe," Agatha corrected.

"Rocko, Roscoe," Lydia waved her hand in the air, "that's not what's important. What's important is that Rocko hired a hotshot reporter from out-of-town to do a complete investigation of the Amelia Dettmer case and the Baileys' role in it. Her reporting was so good, there's talk it might win a Pulitzer Prize!" Lydia waited for Agatha to at least feign interest. "Anyway, it turned out Mr. Bailey had gone to great lengths to get his hands on the trust's money for Lynette. After that came out, he was forced to leave the firm his great grandfather founded and surrender his law license or face being stripped of it and disbarred," her mother said.

"That must be hard on Mrs. Bailey and Lynette."

"Not at all!" Lydia said. "As a result of the exposé Rocko published…."

Roscoe, Agatha thought to herself, Roscoe.

"Mrs. Bailey and her roses got a lot of press. And because of that…." Lydia paused for dramatic effect. "She received scads of invitations to speak on the rose lecture circuit."

"That's great," Agatha said, unaware there was such a thing as a rose lecture circuit and hoping the conversation was over. She wanted to get to The Coffee Shop for a cappuccino to help clear the cobwebs from her head. Still, she couldn't shake the feeling that something was missing. But what?

"Then there's Lynette," Lydia continued. "She got a position in traffic enforcement with the city."

"You mean she became a police officer?" Agatha asked.

"No. She's more like what they used to call a 'meter maid.'"

"I'm glad she's found a job she likes. I didn't think she'd ever forgive me for buying that hat."

"I don't know that she has," Lydia said, "but the citations she's issuing are certainly shaking things up at the courthouse. Marcus Hill's business is booming."

"You haven't said anything about Mr. Bailey? What's he doing?"

"I guess you haven't been to The Coffee Shop."

"I only got in last night," Agatha reminded her mother "so no, I haven't." Lydia remained uncharacteristically quiet. "Well, are you going to tell me about Mr. Bailey?"

"Only because you asked," her mother said. "It turns out that all those times they visited Italy so Mrs. Bailey could study roses, Mr. Bailey took classes in how to brew espresso. Word has it he is a very good barista."

"Interesting," Agatha said. She desperately needed a cappuccino, but she didn't know what she thought about Mr. Bailey serving it up.

"He's making quite a name for himself."

"I'm sure he is," Agatha said, then seized the opportunity the lull in the conversation provided. "Gotta go, now!"

"Wait a minute," her mother said. "Since you're already running errands, you can take a couple of minutes to drop this off at QGARST." Lydia handed Agatha a bag overflowing with odds and ends from the still unfinished decluttering project.

"Can't you do it?" Agatha asked.

"No, I can't," her mother said firmly. "I have to pick up M. Poirot from the groomer, and I won't have time."

M. Poirot, Agatha thought, that's what was missing! The four-legged twelve-pound ball of fur and snarls who absolutely hated her. How could she have forgotten?

But, she didn't have time to give it much thought. After a quick stop at The Coffee Shop for the much needed cappuccino, which, she grudgingly admitted was very good, she went to the library where she and Hank caught up in hushed whispers about what had gone on in her absence.

QGARST, here I come, she thought as she wended her way toward the thrift store.

"Howdy, stranger!" Andrea greeted her.

"We have to stop meeting like this," Agatha teased plopping the bag on the counter. "It was just twelve weeks ago you sold me the hat that changed the course of my life!"

"Time does fly," Andrea said. "Do you remember that motion Mr. Bailey wrote?

"Yes," Agatha said. "I wonder what became of it."

"Nothing is what became of it. Lynette got there too late which turned out to be a good thing."

"How?" Agatha asked, genuinely curious.

"Have you heard about Lynette's new job?"

"I have," Agatha said.

"Well, if she had gotten that motion filed she would have been an accessory to a criminal scheme that her dad had cooked up, but because she got there two minutes too late, the clerk refused to take it. So when she worked out a restitution agreement to repay the trust, she was able to pass the background check for the parking enforcement position."

The bell over the door rang.

"Speak of the devil," Andrea said under her breath.

The click of the high heels Lynette favored had been replaced with the clomp of sturdy work shoes.

"I think that's my cue to exit," she said, winking.

"Better watch where you park," Lynette said, as Agatha beat a path to the door.

"I will."

With her in-town obligations settled, Agatha headed out to Amelia Dettmer's place.

When the rescue came within view, she was astonished at the transformation. The house had been redone from the ground up. There were new windows and a large colorful sign identified the property as the Amelia Dettmer Memorial Animal Rescue.

On the grounds there was a large fenced area with state-of-the-art dog kennels.

"Welcome!" It was Sam walking with a large dog who was crying. "This is Rufus," she said. "He has separation anxiety issues, but we will get him through it," she turned to the pony-sized dog. "Isn't that right, baby?" Rufus looked at Sam with a mixture of adoration and anxiety.

"I had no idea you were such an accomplished dog whisperer," Agatha said.

"A girl's got to keep a few secrets," Sam said winking. "Now come on. You have to take the tour!"

There were new cat houses next to a para-professional clinic where the rescue animals were examined daily and an on-call veterinarian could come to treat the animals on site. Agatha noticed that Sam was as happy in her new role at the Animal Rescue as Agatha was as a crochet designer.

"I need to get home and start work on a new design," Agatha said a few minutes after the tour concluded.

"Oh, you can't go yet!" Sam said. "The whole time you were gone, I tried to think of what I could do to show my appreciation for all you did to save the rescue, and then...."

"And then?" Agatha said.

"And then Miss Marple arrived, and I immediately thought of you!"

This Miss Marple, Agatha learned, was not a fictional character in an Agatha Christie novel—she was a cat. With all of her sleek, black fur, Agatha shuddered to think how much vacuuming she would have to do, but the cat's coat would make her crochet photos "pop."

"So what do you think?" Sam asked.

"I think I'm going to be the proud mistress of a cat named Miss Marple," Agatha said as the cat sidled up to her and began rubbing against her ankles.

While Agatha and Miss Marple got acquainted, Sam disappeared into the front office then quickly reappeared.

"Here are her records," Sam said handing Agatha a stack of papers. "It was really important to find a home where Miss Marple could keep her name. Her owner was a young woman — a knitter in fact — who got her while she was in college, but then she was offered a job with Global Yarns. She didn't want to leave her cat, but it was the job offer of a lifetime."

And, that, Agatha understood all too well.

As she picked up Miss Marple and all of her things, she gazed thoughtfully at her new housemate. Despite the many skills Agatha had picked up at The Agency, she could not see into the future.

But still, as she looked at Miss Marple, she sensed that exciting days were soon to come.

Acknowledgements

I owe a debt of thanks to my first grade teacher, Mrs. Sullivan, who made me the reader that I am. And thanks is also due my third grade teacher, Mrs. Cook, who seated me next to Laurie Noble. Laurie was (and is) a wonderful friend, and it was her older sister, Betsy, who let me "borrow" her Nancy Drew books so many decades ago.

I also owe a debt of gratitude to the writers I studied with at Warren Wilson College: Kevin McIlvoy (who, like so many, is gone too soon), Judith Grossman, Michael Martone, and Geoffrey Wolff. They were generous with their time and knowledge and helped me become a better writer.

I began working on this story in earnest when my mother found an online course, Mystery Writing 101, through the Durham County Library, and in that course, I learned just how much I didn't know. Thanks is also due to Dr. Carlotta Berry who, when I had given up on this manuscript, invited me to participate in her writing accountability group where I took an exceedingly messy 3rd draft and worked (and reworked) it until it was no longer so messy.

Thank you to my early readers—Thomas Neuburger and Janine M. Ziermann—both of whom gave me comments and guidance that allowed me to make *The Secret of the Old Cloche* the story it could be.

Thank you to all of my crochet peeps who are the best friends anyone could have—with special acknowledgement to the real Andrea Walker—there's no one with whom I'd rather go to a martini bar to grab a coffee.

Thank you to the incomparable, Felicia Cedillos, who took the many threads of what I thought I wanted and wove it into a delightful book cover.

And to each of my three children who have each changed me in ways I will never know, thank you.

And last, but most certainly not least, thank you to my husband, Jordan Jones, for his insights, his encouragement, and his willingness to go all of the extra miles need to get this project done.

Made in the USA
Columbia, SC
06 February 2023

11264560R00122